With its lessons about the true meaning of family, this book will resonate with fans of novels such as Shelby Van Pelt's *Remarkably Bright Creatures*. Logan is an inspirational character. His pursuit of the truth about his mother will encourage readers to remember that pursuing their goals and dreams in spite of the odds is important. The protagonist also possesses a philosophical nature which makes him wise beyond his years. For example, he states that he "left a shimmering ocean with sounds and smells that made me feel alive to come to a place with sounds and smells that made me feel out of place." As he leaves one place to find another to call "home," his experiences communicate the significance of place in one's life. For adults and young adults alike, this book is a unique page-turning take on the subjects of adoption and family. **–Nicole Yurcaba, *US Review of Books***

Kim has written a lovely YA story about a teenager setting off across the country to find answers about his adoption. I loved all the compassionate, funny characters he met along the way, and her descriptions of the places he traveled made me want to set off on a road trip myself–not a surprise given the adventure-loving author. Definitely adding it to the classroom library when it comes out in August! –**Maddy Ryen, English Language Development teacher**

To Whom It May Concern follows the once-in-a-lifetime adventure of thirteen-year-old, Logan, who discovers he is adopted and runs away to find his birth mother and the answers to his questions. Along the way, he meets a bevy of colorful personalities and learns that life is full of unconventional circumstances and that mothers who choose to give up their children for adoption do so for a multitude of reasons. As an adoptee myself, I can relate the urge to run away to find answers to the situation that led to my adoption; both my mom and I are adopted, so I know that questioning is a common practice among all adoptees. –**Alex Kultgen, adoptee**

TO WHOM IT MAY CONCERN:

TO WHOM IT MAY CONCERN:

THEY TELL ME YOU'RE MY MOTHER

KIM ORENDOR

IDUN

Nashville, Tennessee

Idun is an imprint of W. Brand Publishing.

j.brand@wbrandpub.com

www.wbrandpub.com

Cover design by designchik.net

Publisher's Note: This is a work of fiction. Names, characters, places, and incidents are a product of the author's imagination. Locales and public names are sometimes used for atmospheric purposes. Any resemblance to actual people, living or dead, or to businesses, companies, events, institutions, or locales is completely coincidental.

To Whom It May Concern / Kim Orendor–1st edition

Paperback ISBN: 978-1-956906-55-4

eBook ISBN: 978-1-956906-56-1

Kindle

Library of Congress Number: 2023902701

CONTENTS

To family

PROLOGUE

TO WHOM IT MAY CONCERN, THEY TELL ME
YOU'RE MY MOTHER.

The words felt heavy as I forced myself to write them. I'm Jill Fisher's son Logan, or at least I was until a few days ago.

"Are you okay in there, young man?"

Even behind the locked office door, the lady from the front desk hounded me. Her perfume sought me out from under the door.

"I'm fine," I said. I'm not really, but what's one more lie now? I'm not sure I'll ever be fine again.

It was supposed to be my cousin standing here. He's the odd one in the family. If anyone was adopted, it should have been him.

But turns out . . . it was me.

I found out the day before my thirteenth birthday: June 10, 1995. Ironically, my cousin John Michael told me. I knew he was trouble when he wouldn't answer to just plain "John." It was John Michael or nothing. He was definitely my aunt's boy; otherwise, she would have tried to give him back a long time ago. At least, I would have asked for a refund.

John Michael was the rock in my shoe. Not even the nice kind that plops out when you slip off your shoe and turn it upside down. No, John Michael was the rock you had to beat out.

He was the one kid I never wanted at my parties and always the first one to arrive. It seemed fitting for my thirteenth birthday that he showed up an entire day early. I should have known my world was about to fall apart.

"Young man," the lady said in hushed tones. "Are you okay? Do you need any help?"

Did I need help? Sure. I'm thousands of miles from home in a hospital lobby with no money, no family that I know of, and a smelly nurse. Yes, I need help.

"I'm fine, really. I'm almost done."

If done meant writing the first line, then I was nearly done. What do you write to someone you've never met? What do you say when the person you've never met turns out to be your mother?

The first line was easy: *To whom it may concern, they tell me you're my mother.* Should that be who? Never mind. Maybe she's as bad at grammar as I am.

It was the rest of the note that was the trouble. I didn't want to write it. I didn't want to be anybody's son but Jill's. I thought she was my real mom. She was the woman who raised me; bandaged my knees, elbows, and forehead; calmed my fears; and encouraged me to dream. But it turns out, she's not my mother.

Jill and David—the man formerly known as Dad—lied to me. An untold lie, but a lie is a lie they taught me. I wanted the truth. I needed the truth. I was having trouble facing the truth.

"Young man. You've been in there a long time."

Time. That's what started the whole thing.

"I get Grandfather's gold pocket watch," John Michael said. A stupid old watch. I was now standing in a hospital office in Nowhere, Kansas, because of a watch on a chain.

I glanced at my watch. Jill and David gave it to me for my tenth birthday. I unbuckled the band and glanced at the face that reminded me, "Don't Be Too Late." It was 2:55. Setting the watch gently on the counter, I pushed the unfinished note in my pocket, unlocked the door, and stepped out into the lobby.

"I'll come back tomorrow," I said, sidestepping the lady but not her perfume that followed me down the hall.

Outside I watched cotton-candy clouds float across the sun. At home, the sun would slip in and out of the puffs of fluff and dip into the ocean. There's no ocean here. I miss the way the sun reflects on the Pacific. The way it melts into the water like an after-dinner mint, slowly, sweetly, smoothly. I miss the smell of the ocean. Kansas has its smells but nothing like the scent that drifts along the California coast.

I want to go home, but I'm not sure where that is anymore.

CHAPTER 1

"**L**ogan. Get the door."

Mom's voice echoed down the hallway. I snagged my sandals from the end of the bed and ran down the stairs. Mom always had me answer the door the day before my birthday. My grandparents on her side usually sent a large package in the mail. Opening the door to see the mailman straining under its weight was half the fun of the present for me.

This year, however, the package from Grandfather— he believed in "formality"—would be small.

Leaping over the last three steps, I grabbed the doorknob and swung open the door. My heart sank.

"Oh, it's you."

"Happy day-before-your-birthday day, Logan," said Aunt Patty as she locked me in one of her death-grip hugs. "This is going to be a great party."

I nodded, knowing in my heart that it wasn't even going to be a good day anymore.

"John Michael don't be rude." Aunt Patty grabbed him behind the neck and pulled him forward. "What do you have to say?"

"Happy birthday, Logan," he said with as much enthusiasm as I felt about him being there.

"Thanks."

The awkward moment was cut short as Mom came to the front door.

"Patty? You're here early. A *whole* day early."

"Well, I just thought I could help."

Mom smiled the way she does when Dad volunteers to "help."

"That's so thoughtful of you." Mom rubbed her hands together. It was her secret sign. I'm not even sure she knew she did it.

When she didn't want to tell the whole truth, she'd say a half-truth and rub her hands together. It was as if she were trying to squash the truth in her hands. She called Aunt Patty "thoughtful," but I'm sure if she'd finished the sentence, it would have been, "That's so thoughtful of you, but you really shouldn't have because you drive me crazy."

Truth, at least Mom's version, always had a dark side that must be hidden or, at the least, ground in your palms.

2

I watched the two women walk to the kitchen. They were arguing about my birthday lunch menu before they'd taken five steps. Poor Mom.

With John Michael in the house, I no longer wanted to stick around and wait for the mailman.

"I'm going to the pool. Be back later." I didn't care about my present. I just wanted to get away.

"Take John Michael with you," called the voice from the kitchen.

She had to be kidding. He wasn't even dressed for the water. I'd only seen him in shorts a handful of times our entire lives, and today he was wearing the unofficial uniform of inlanders: khaki pants and a polo shirt.

"I'm not sure I want John Michael at some public pool," Aunt Patty said.

She and Mom were now standing in the archway, looking down the hallway at us.

"I would prefer not to go to a pool," John Michael said.

"It's not really a pool. It's the ocean," I said.

"Then I really would prefer not to go."

He would "prefer not to go," and I would prefer he stay. Case closed. "Okay. See ya," I said, grabbing my skim board.

"Logan."

Mom's tone stopped me in my tracks. I didn't even have to look at her to know she was shaking her head. It was the same tone she used on me when I tried to ditch my little brother, Dayton. I took a half-step backward and leaned the board against the wall.

"What would you prefer to do?"

"Do you have any new video games?"

I nodded and started up the stairs. It was odd to me that John Michael's favorite Nintendo 64 game was wave racing. He never wanted to go in the water, but he loved that game.

He talked about the car ride while he played. He said something about cows and oaks and fault lines. I wasn't listening to him. I slid open the window and listened for the ocean.

My room faced the mighty Pacific. Technically, it faced the Pacific View Apartments. No matter how far left or right I leaned out my window, I couldn't see the ocean, but I knew it was there.

"You want to play, Logan?"

"No, thanks." I didn't want to hit buttons; I wanted to hit the beach.

The surf was sweet today, and I'd already missed numerous excellent waves waiting for a present. My ears caught the crashing of the waves and soon my heart was beating in time to their cadence. The sun warmed me and a gentle breeze stirred through the window to cool me, just a touch. The rolling waves drowned out all noise. The floor under my feet felt cold and grainy. I could see the wave break, churning up foam and pushing the thin layer of water for skim boards to glide on.

"I gotta go. You want to join me, great. If not, playing the reverse level is pretty cool."

I didn't even wait to hear John Michael's preference. I had my board and was halfway down the driveway before the door slammed.

CHAPTER 2

God's pool. That's what Dad called the ocean.

It's what his dad—who preferred to be "just plain ol' Grandpa"—called it.

"The sad thing," Grandpa would say, "is that God's so big that when He puts His toe in here, penguins get knocked off ice floes way over yonder."

It seemed unfair to me that God could create such an awesome ocean and not be able to enjoy it. I made it my mission in life to enjoy it for Him.

Running across the frontage road, I exchanged the hard asphalt for soft sand. A most-excellent exchange in my opinion. Without losing a step, I slipped out of my sandals. There was a sudden burst of heat on my soles. Then just as quickly my feet were on wet sand, cooled by an outgoing wave.

"Dude. We didn't think you were going to make it."

Blue was my best friend. His parents were third-generation beach drifters, who finally settled down. His mother sold hand-made jewelry at the pier, and his dad carved sea creatures out of driftwood.

They stopped drifting just before Blue was born and lived in an old apartment complex—Blue called it a community. I enjoyed visiting with all the people who lived there and helping pick fruits and vegetables from the courtyard garden.

"Where you been, man?" Dayton chimed in. "Did the package come from Grandfather?"

"No, but John Michael showed up."

"Sorry, Dude," said Blue, patting me on the shoulder. "That's one present you're going to want to return."

I laughed, and they joined me.

"Okay," I said. "No more wasting time."

Blue and Dayton stepped aside and let me skim the next wave. I tossed the board ahead of me and ran after it. To the tourists, I was just some crazy kid chasing a piece of plywood covered in graffiti.

To me it was heaven.

The freedom of gliding on water refreshed my cousin-weary head. However, just when I thought my head was all clear, I saw John Michael tiptoeing through the sea grass to the sand. He sat down on the edge of the beach, took off his shoes, slipped his socks inside each leather foot trap and rolled up his pants to his knees.

He timidly touched his toe to the sand and jumped to the other foot. He high stepped his way across the beach to where the waves eased up the shore.

"Would you like to try?" I asked John Michael, knowing the answer was "No."

"I prefer to watch."

"Not a problem."

Not even John Michael could take the joy out of skimming across the beach.

I worked my way farther down the beach to avoid talking with him too much. The lack of shadows told me it was getting close to lunch time, so I headed back to John Michael, who was talking with Dayton.

"Logan. He said a package came for you right after you left. He said it was small."

"Really?"

John Michael, as matter of fact as always, said, "Yes. It was about the size of an orange."

"A Valencia or navel?" asked Blue.

"Does it matter?" John Michael said.

I'm sure Blue would have gone into a long explanation on the history of the varieties of citrus and the subtle differences. He knew more about plants than anyone I knew. But this was no time for a lesson.

"It's okay, Blue. His mother buys their produce at a store."

Blue shook his head.

"I bet it's the watch," Dayton said.

"No, it's not," John Michael said with a great deal of conviction.

"How do you know?" Dayton shot back.

"Because my mother told me."

"Why would Grandfather tell Aunt Patty what he got Logan for his birthday?"

"He didn't," said John Michael, who was now starting to get a touch of pink around his ears. "Oh, never mind. I'm going back."

Blue and Dayton ran ahead. I slipped on my sandals and waited for John Michael. He brushed the sand off his feet, careful to sweep between his toes twice before putting on his socks. He dumped and re-dumped his shoes. He unrolled his pants and tried to smooth out the wrinkles. He just didn't seem to know how to have fun. And his inability to have fun was like kryptonite to my own good time.

"It's not the watch," he said as he stood up and wiped the sand off the seat of his pants.

"Fine. Let's just get lunch."

I thought the conversation was over but should have known better. John Michael wouldn't let a conversation end until he was sure he had the best word, not the last word, but the word with the most impact. I let him win these games. They meant nothing to me but appeared to make him happy.

"You want to know *how* I know?"

"Not really."

When we got to the house, Blue and Dayton were sitting under a tree in the front yard. They were eating sandwiches and washing them down with lemonade.

"Man, you two are slow," Dayton forced out of a mouth full of PB&J.

"Be quiet," I said. "You're rude for running off and leaving a guest."

I'd barely finished the sentence when I remembered running out of my room, leaving John Michael alone with the video game. "Sorry for ditching you earlier."

"It's okay," he said. "Sorry, I'm getting the watch."

CHAPTER 3

I waited until we were back outside with our sandwiches and drinks before asking John Michael about the watch. I didn't ask inside because Grandfather's watch was a hot topic between my mom and her sister. No need adding more drama to my birthday.

"Not that I really care, but why do you think you're getting the watch?"

"My mother said so."

"My mommy said so. My mommy said so," Dayton mimicked.

"Dayton, stop it. John Michael be glad you don't have a little brother."

Dayton made a face and leaned against the tree. He started talking with Blue.

"What did Aunt Patty tell you?" I asked.

"She said for me not to worry that Grandfather's watch was to go to the first-born grandson."

"Then you should worry because Logan is eight months older than you," Dayton piped in.

I shot him my best big-brother stare.

"What? It's true," Dayton said.

"It's true Logan's older," said John Michael, leaning toward me and lowering his voice. "But you're not the first-born. Mom said adopted children don't count in the family bloodline."

Adopted?

Aunt Patty told John Michael I was adopted just so he'd think he'd get Grandfather's watch?

"That's a fascinating little story John Michael, but I'm just as much a part of this family as you are."

"We'll see when you open your present tomorrow," he said as he got up and went back into the house.

"Your cousin seems uptight. He needs to spend more time with his shoes off," said Blue, wiggling his well-tanned toes in the grass.

"Dayton, where'd Mom put my present from Grandfather?"

"In the hall closest. Want me to get it?"

"Yeah, but don't let anyone see."

I couldn't believe Aunt Patty would say such lies to try and make John Michael happy. I couldn't believe a watch would mean so much. I'd seen it once before at my grandparent's house.

It looked like any other gold pocket watch. It had my grandfather's initials T.F.R.—Theodore Franklin Rollins—engraved on the outside. On the inside was Psalm 45:17, "I will make your name to be remembered in all generations."

The whole thing seemed a bit old-fashioned to me, besides it wasn't even waterproof. I didn't have that many pants with pockets, either. What did I need with a silly gold watch?

I didn't need a watch, but I didn't need a cousin stirring up trouble either. If Dayton told Mom what John Michael had said, I knew she'd be just as upset with Aunt Patty's lies.

No, to keep the peace, I'd do some investigating of my own.

Dayton came out with nothing in his hands but a bulge under his T-shirt. He slipped the package out from under his shirt, holding it in front of me.

"Valencia. That's definitely the size of a Valencia orange."

"Thanks, Blue." I took the package and worked the tape like the professional un-wrapper I am. I pulled the paper off without ripping it and held the box in my hand. There was no writing on the box to indicate a store. It felt about the right weight for the watch.

Dayton and Blue both crept toward me. It was as if the box was drawing us all closer. I could feel Dayton's breath on my arm. "Give. Me. Room."

They backed up a bit. I inched up the lid.

"Whoa! That's awesome," Blue said.

The Swiss Army knife sat nestled in the box. A block "L" was carved near the top. I looked at Dayton. Our eyes met, and for the first time my brother had nothing to say.

CHAPTER 4

I'm not sure how long I walked that afternoon. I blindly followed Dayton and Blue back to the beach and then kept walking.

"Where you going, Logan?"

"Dunno," I said without turning around. "I need to think."

Maybe the knife was a decoy gift. Grandfather knew I was sneaky. Maybe my real present had been sent weeks earlier.

No, Dayton wasn't that good at keeping secrets. The longest he'd ever been able to go without tattling was three days, twelve hours and fifteen minutes, or forty-five minutes short of me being able to go to an unsupervised sleep over.

So, I had three days plus of him keeping quiet about John Michael's secret, but I wouldn't need that long. Family would start talking tomorrow as soon as I opened the box from my grandparents.

I loved the knife. It would be perfect on camping trips and hikes. It was what I really wanted for my birthday. Then how come I couldn't stop thinking about that watch?

"Logan, what are you doing this far down the beach so late?"

For the first time in a while, I really looked around. I was no longer on my stretch of beach.

"Hey, Rachel. I was just getting some thinking done and lost track of sand."

Rachel was a permanent fixture on the third bench from Sonny's Surf Shop. She had a nice home, but she said she felt "more at home outside helping other people".

Sometimes she'd make extra sandwiches and pass them out to anyone who was hungry. She even gave them to Blue and me once. They were good.

There was a catch. If you took a sandwich, you had to promise to go to church with her. Blue and I were the only blonde people in the church, but it was fun. It was more exciting than the church we normally went to with my family. Rachel's pastor spoke—mostly shouted—and the people shouted back.

He talked about God and about Jesus and about Jesus being the Truth and the Truth setting us free. And the people said, "Amen." Every now and then Blue and I would throw out an "Amen."

I liked being around Rachel because she only spoke the truth. The whole truth with no hand rubbing. When she said something was good, it was good. And she'd tell the bad stuff, too.

Once, I hadn't showered for more than a day and just figured the ocean would clean me. Rachel told me to "get myself home and get clean." Of course, she gave me a hug—stinky and all—before sending me on my way.

Yeah, I liked "getting lost" on Rachel's beach.

"Tomorrow's the big day," she said, bringing my thoughts back to today.

"Yep. The big one-three."

"I'm actually glad you're here because I thought I'd have to give this as a belated present." Rachel reached into her canvas bag. An unruly strand of gray hair fell out of her hat and onto her cheek. She pulled out a paper bag that she had decorated with colored markers. In handwriting that resembled my grandma's, she wrote, "Happy Birthday, dear Logan."

"You didn't have to get me anything."

"I know, child. Now, open it."

I turned the bag around in my hand, careful to look at every side, to see every detail Rachel put on the bag. I unfolded the top, glanced up at Rachel—she was smiling and motioning for me to hurry. I put my hand in the bag and knew instantly what it was. The well-worn side contrasted with the bumps and curves. It was a beautiful shell, with blues and reds and oranges.

"I love it, Rachel. It's like holding the sunset." I wrapped my arms around her and whispered. "It's beautiful. Just like you."

"There's no more gifts even for sweet things like that," she said pushing me gently away. "Now, get on home before your momma starts to worry."

The top of the sun was just about to settle into the ocean. I knew I could be home before the sun went down if I ran on the road. It was the fastest way, but it would mean missing a sunset. I ran as fast as I could on the sand and hit my beach as the tip of the sun slipped away, leaving the sky crimson and orange.

I was going to be late, but it was worth it. For a few precious moments, Rachel helped me forget about the watch.

That time was over.

CHAPTER 5

It was the quietest dinner ever at our house.

Small talk was all anyone could muster. We talked about the weather, the surf, the heat, and the party.

"Are you excited Logan?" Aunt Patty asked.

"Yeah. It should be a great day. Forecast is sunny skies, light breeze, and perfect waves."

I was more than willing to wait for my party. It was harder waiting to get back to the beach. I'd convinced Mom to have the party at the beach. One massive picnic with all my favorite foods, favorite friends, and one annoying cousin. What more could a boy want?

John Michael's comment continued to eat at me. I stared at Dad's features. I had his eyes. Everyone always told me that. "Eyes so blue as to make the sky jealous," Grandpa would say. I had my mother's smile, not too flashy with a slight dimple on the left. It was "a smile to break hearts," according to Grandma.

But it wasn't my eyes and mouth that was causing the real trouble. It was my heart being crushed. Every second that passed, it felt tighter. I imagined myself in the grip of King Kong. The more I thought about not being me, the more he tightened his grip. I tried to push his fingers off my chest, but it was useless. The lack of oxygen made me lightheaded. I felt my heart beating in my head. The room started spinning and then went black.

"Logan. Logan, wake up."

Mom was calling me and shaking me by the shoulders. I opened my eyes and looked up from the floor to see my family—or supposed family—hovering over me.

"You fainted and fell out of the chair. Are you feeling okay?"

"I'm fine, Mom," I said, pushing myself up into a sitting position.

"Here, put this on your head." Dad handed me an ice pack.

"I don't need it, honest." I tried to push it away, but he placed it just above the base of my skull. The cold sent another shock through my body. By the time I got used to the temperature, my nerves were misfiring because of the pain as he applied pressure.

Maybe I wasn't fine.

At least the pain in my head took away the pressure from my heart.

Grandpa taught me to look for silver linings, while Grandfather taught me to line my pockets with silver. Why did I want a watch from him?

"I'm going to go to bed," I said.

"I'm not sure that's a good idea, Jill," Aunt Patty said. "He could have a concussion."

"I'm sure he's all right," Mom said. "But I'll be up to check on you later, Logan."

"G'night."

I passed my boards that were leaning against the wall on my way upstairs. I ran my fingers along the edge and over the top, there was still a coolness there. The light smell of surf lingered in the corner. It calmed my spirit.

Sleep was not what I was after. I plopped on top of the covers, aggravating the bump on the back of my head. Fluffing the pillow just right fixed the problem. I stared at the ceiling. I had carefully created a spectacular display with surfing pictures, travel posters, and calendars. I could imagine myself hanging ten on the pipeline, or skimming along in Mexico, or just kicking back on the beach in any month.

"Logan." Mom knocked gently twice.

"Come in."

"Just wanted to check on you before we went to bed," said Mom as she and Dad came into the room. "Is everything all right?"

Go ahead, lie, Logan, say "Yes" and send them away, I thought. It was the last rational thought I'd have for a while.

"Am I adopted?"

CHAPTER 6

Mom and Dad exchanged glances and feeble smiles. I saw the same reaction just before they told me I was getting a little brother, I had to have my tonsils out, and my dog Crest had been hit by a car.

No good news had ever followed those looks. None.

Tonight would be no different.

"Why do you ask?" said Mom as her and Dad walked over to sit on my bed.

I propped myself up against the headboard, making more room for both of them. It also put me closer to eye level. Grandpa always said, "Don't take bad news lying down."

"Am I?" I asked.

"Logan, where is this coming from?" Mom reached for my foot, and I pulled it up close to me. She wasn't going to get out of answering the question with a foot massage.

"Does Grandfather's watch go to the first-born grandson on his thirteenth birthday?"

"Yes," Mom said. "But what does that have to do with . . ."

"He gave me a pocket knife."

"Logan, you looked?" Mom said, her voice rising. "David, tell him he shouldn't have looked."

"You know the boy looks. Everyone knows he looks."

" 'The boy?' Now, I'm the boy. It's true?"

Dad reached out his large suntanned arms and pulled me close to him. He held me firm. We were inches apart, sky-blue eyes to sky-blue eyes.

"I call you 'boy' because you *are* a boy. I also call you 'son' because you *are* my son."

If he had stopped there, life may have gone on as normal. A few minutes with John Michael to teach him a lesson or two, and all would be right. But Dad didn't stop there.

His fingers no longer held me fast but started to tremble. Tears welled in his eyes. He glanced at Mom, and she began to tear up as well. She nodded, and he turned back to look at me. "Logan, you weren't supposed to find out this way."

"It's true?" I half-whispered, half-cried. I didn't want to cry. I wanted to be angry. "Why didn't you tell me? Why? . . . Who is? . . . What else don't I know?"

"There's really not much to know," Dad said.

"Not much to know? Are you kidding me?" I pushed him away. "You're not my parents. Dayton's not my brother. John Michael's not my cousin—that's good news, but still. How can you say there's not much to know?"

"Son, that was probably the wrong thing to say. I'm sorry."

"Don't call me 'son,'" I said as I flung my legs over the side of the bed. "You're not my dad or my mom. From now on, you're David and Jill."

My words were brutal. I saw Jill's shoulders convulse with crying. It was too late; I was on a roll.

"Who are my parents? Don't tell me I'm from The Valley, please. Do you know anything? I want to know everything you know."

David slowly got up, grabbed the chair from my desk and slid it in front of me. Jill inched her way up the bed toward me. She stopped shaking and dried her eyes.

"You were born in Kansas," David said.

"Kansas?" It was worse than I could have imagined. "Why didn't you tell me?"

"Your mother was a young runaway," Jill said, massaging her palm with her thumb. "She left you at the

Fort Scott hospital with a note, asking to please find you a good home."

"We hadn't been able to have children and were looking to adopt," said David, who also started to rub his hands. This must be some cover up. "Our friend called us when he heard the story. We seemed to be a perfect match."

"Normally, Logan, there would have been mounds of paperwork," Jill said. "But things went so smoothly, so quickly, we knew you were meant to be ours."

"If you felt that way, why didn't you tell me sooner? Were you ashamed?" I looked back and forth between them. Both were doing a lot of hand wringing. "Why did I have to learn from John Michael? Why didn't you tell me?"

"We wanted to, but it never seemed to be the right time," Jill said. "We almost did several times, but then we never could find the words."

"Logan, you're adopted. Those are all the words you needed," I said. "Bobby Thompson's parents didn't have any trouble telling him he was adopted."

"Bobby Thompson is Korean, and his parents are white," David said. "It's obvious he's adopted."

"Does everyone in the family know?" I asked, not caring about what was obvious.

"Yes, except for Dayton," Jill said. "But it's never been a big deal. Everyone still loves you like family Logan. You should know that."

"Not Grandfather," I said. I didn't tell them Dayton knew about the watch. I could have my secrets, too. "Grandfather doesn't see me as a part of the family. That stupid old watch. I hope John Michael chokes on it."

"Logan."

"Can I be alone now? Please."

Jill reached to hug me. I let her. David ran his hand along my head. I winced when he hit the bump.

"Sorry, champ."

I nodded. He leaned down and kissed the top of my head, and they left.

As soon as they shut the door, I walked to my desk, turned on the computer, and pulled up a search engine.

"Kansas. Where the heck is Kansas?"

CHAPTER 7

The Sunflower State.

Sunflowers? What did I know about sunflowers? I knew palm trees, ice plant, and dunes.

Staring at the images on the screen there was nothing special about Kansas. It was lost in the middle of the United States. Nowhere near an ocean, not even close to water.

I stared at myself in the mirror. Blonde hair? Check. Blue eyes? Check. Tan? Check. Athletic, outgoing, adventurous? Check, check, check.

In the mirror, I saw my backpack hanging on my chair. A blue-and-gold button caught my eye. The writing was backwards in the reflection, but I knew what it said. I had worn it like a badge of honor since the day I got it at the county fair: Made in California. It was the cornerstone of my someday-to-be-launched X-Games career: California's Golden Boy brings home the gold.

Now, it was a lie. I was some freakish transplant from Kansas.

There must be more to the story otherwise David and Jill would have told me sooner. What are they hiding?

I plucked the badge from the pack and dropped it into the trash. I drifted off to sleep thinking of Kansas, counting sunflower seeds.

Noise from downstairs woke me. I was usually up with the sun ready to start the day. I didn't want this day to start, but I sure wanted it over.

David, Jill, and I exchanged "Hi's" in the kitchen, but I wasn't going to give them a smile. They'd have to wait and see it when I put on the soon-to-be Academy Award-nominated performance of a lifetime later that afternoon.

"Happy Birthday, Logan," said Dayton, pouncing on me from behind.

I grabbed him and wrestled him to the floor. Making him laugh was my greatest pleasure in life next to surfing. His giggle was infectious, and I was really hoping to catch it today. He laughed, and I acted. It wasn't working. The California magic wouldn't work on a Kansas mind. My life was over.

TO WHOM IT MAY CONCERN:

The carefully hand-picked guests—except for John Michael—enjoyed the morning surf. We left all the presents at home. Jill said it would be a good break to come back and enjoy the shade for a while. I protested when the suggestion was first made days ago, but today it would work to my advantage.

We were supposed to be at the beach until one o'clock. It was now ten. It would only give me a three-hour head start, but if I played it right, it would be all I needed.

"Dayton. Dayton, come here."

He ran from a pack of friends.

"This better be important," he said, hands on his hips.

"I've got to go back to the house. I want to change boards."

"Liar."

Was he on to me? "Why do you say that?"

"You want to go look at what everyone got you, so you can pick out the order to open the presents."

On any other day he would be right. In the past, I'd sneak in the house, unwrap everything, and then plan the most dramatic order of opening. It was sneaky but fun.

"Okay, so you know my plan. I also want to go see Rachel. You know how she always has something special for us."

Dayton nodded and closed his eyes. "Yeah. She's the best. All right, I'll cover for you. But don't be too late."

"Thanks Dayton, you're the best bro ..." The word caught in my throat. He wasn't my brother, not really.

"Dude, no matter what John Michael says, you're my big brother. Don't ever forget that," he said, punching me in the arm. "Now, go find out what you got for your birthday."

CHAPTER 8

Face to face with a mound of presents and cards, I was tempted to just rip into things but that would tip off David and Jill and cut down on my getaway time.

During the night it came to me, I had to get to Fort Scout, Scott, Something, Kansas, and find out what David and Jill were hiding. I had to find out who my real parents were. Did they have blonde hair, blue eyes, and a dimple? Did they know how to surf? Better question, had they ever seen the surf?

If I wasn't Logan Fisher, surfer, skateboarder, part-time student, and full-time adventurer, who was I? The answer was halfway across the country in Kansas. The way to get there was right in front of me.

I told everyone coming to my party that I was looking to buy a new board and that cash was the preferred gift this season. Green was my favorite color.

Most took my suggestion to heart since the number of cards was staggering. The best part was my friends didn't even lick the envelopes.

If there had been time to stop and read the cards, I would have sent out a mental thank you to each person, but there wasn't. A fifty-dollar bill fell out of one card, and I did sneak a peek at that name, "God bless, Joe." Joe was a hard-core surfer and knew how much a great board would cost me. Being a true friend, he was helping me get the best. Of course today, that meant the best seat on a bus headed east.

A few cards came with checks, which normally would be as good as cash, except I didn't have a way to get to the bank, and I'm sure Jill wasn't going to drive me there, and then to the bus station. So, I did the next best thing.

I gathered the checks and found Jill's purse and David's stash in his sock drawer. I took the money and left the checks. With several hundred dollars in my pocket, I packed a few clothes, snacks, and my MP3 in a backpack, and rode my bicycle two miles to the bus depot.

The main bus terminal was crowded. People sat or sprawled on benches throughout the lobby area, waiting for their busses, or to pick up people on the next bus.

A sign informed me that minors under sixteen-years-of-age needed to be with a parent or guardian or have a note from a parent or guardian saying who was picking them up at the other end of the line. This may take a little more work than I thought.

Now, it's just two hours until everyone was supposed to head back to the house. However, by now people know that I'm not around and may be asking questions. My ace in the hole is Jill and David will be willing to give me space today because of the bombshell they dropped on me.

An elderly lady carrying three more bags than she has arms stumbled through the door by me. I quickly grabbed a couple bags to lighten her load.

"Thank you so much," she said with just the hint of a Southern accent. "You are too kind."

"Just being the gentleman my parents raised me to be," I said, flashing her a dimpled smile. "Where are you headed?"

"Fort Smith, Arkansas."

"You're kidding," I said, setting the bags down. "I'm heading there, too."

It was just a bit of a lie. I was trying to get to a Fort and Kansas takes up most of Arkansas.

"How about I get our tickets, and you just sit here?"

"Oh, God bless you."

"I think He just has."

I walked to the counter and ordered two tickets to Fort Smith, Arkansas "for me and my grandma." I'd worry about how to get to where I was actually headed later.

Turns out my "grandma's" name is Delores and she just wrapped up a visit with her real grandchildren in Anaheim. She'd spent three weeks in Southern California hitting all the hot spots and was now headed home.

She was "pleased as punch" to be traveling with me and couldn't wait to meet my grandma in Arkansas. I let this lie slip because for all I knew I really did have a grandma in Arkansas or Nebraska for that matter.

It's odd how when no one is your family that anyone could be.

We rolled out of Los Angeles at 12:30 p.m. headed east. The bus was cramped and smelled like my gym locker on a really warm day. The bus had a magic spell on Delores and everyone else over sixty years old, they were asleep before the bus hit the outskirts of the city.

TO WHOM IT MAY CONCERN:

At least while she was sleeping, I didn't have to come up with any more lies.

Watching the world go by through a water-streaked window was not that entertaining. It was amazing how fast everything became so dry. The rounded mountains were covered in golden grass and scrub oaks. The only thing that broke up the scene were rock formations that randomly jutted out of the ground.

Someone behind me is listening to hip-hop—I actually feel the bass more than hear it, while classical music is escaping from the headset of someone in front of me. The forces collide inside my head like competing waves. Suddenly, they're both drowned out by the engine's noise as it strains to pull the bus up the mountain. I pull out my MP3 player to clear my head.

Cars fly past us. Most people keep looking straight ahead. Occasionally, someone my age will look up at me. We exchange half-smiles, neither one of us really where we want to be.

Just a few hours out of the city and my world is on its head. There are horses and cows grazing in the fields. There are signs on the freeway indicating a town is approaching, but when we get there, it's a few buildings, a gas station, and a hamburger stand.

We weren't slated to stop for a while, so I dug into my snacks. Delores shifted in her seat.

"Billy, dear, don't wander off," she whispered.

"I'm not Billy, and there's no place to wander."

She shifted again, and her breathing became deep. She was talking in her sleep.

I went back to looking out the window. There were all sorts of wildflowers growing on the edge of the highway. They were tangled by the gusts of wind that followed the cars. There were blues, pinks, and yellows. Lots of yellows.

"Hey, mom, look at all the pretty yellow flowers," came a girlish voice from the front of the bus.

"They're sunflowers," a lady said.

Sunflowers, so that's what they looked like in the wild. I'd only seen the seeds in packs at the store. Something told me I was going to see a lot more before the journey was done.

CHAPTER 9

The bus jerked to a stop in front of the station. I'm not sure what the name of the town is since the city-limit sign was a mix of yellow and red paintball splats.

I wasn't interested in its real name anyway. I was interested in getting some fresh air. The lack of good smells on the bus drove me for the exit as soon as the warden opened the door. The bus driver's name badge read "Bob," but warden fit. He controlled my comings and goings. His massive frame overhung the driver's seat on three sides. I'm sure he would have oozed over all four except for the backrest.

"We leave in fifteen minutes," he called after me.

It wasn't long, but it would have to do.

The high-desert air robbed me of any oxygen I had left in my lungs. A couple of deep breaths and I was back to full. The air was warm and dry, nothing like the sticky sweet air of home.

My leg muscles slowly remembered how to function after being trapped so long on the bus. I walked the long way around the station and found the bathroom. I hadn't convinced myself to use the bathroom on the bus. I'd never used a bathroom on a plane either. There were too many horror stories of people being stuck inside or worse being splashed by the toilet contents when a bus hit a pothole. Blue said they were myths, but I wasn't going to take any chances.

The only person in the station, which was primarily a diner that served breakfast twenty-four hours a day, was the waitress. Apparently getting scrambled eggs whenever you wanted was not that big of a draw.

"A little slow?" I said.

She nodded and started wiping down the counter.

The warden hit the horn, and I raced back to my moving prison. The movement of people on and off the bus helped circulate the air a bit. It was now more of a library smell, like musty paper.

The town quickly vanished as we pulled away.

"Grandma" moved across the aisle and now a boy about my age sat next to me.

"Your grandma said I should sit here," he said as I crawled over him to get to the window.

"Great," I said, looking out the window.

"My name's Alexander. But everyone calls me Alex. What's yours?"

I glanced over at him. The only thing brighter than his smile was the orange Tennessee T-shirt he wore.

"Logan," I said with as little enthusiasm as I could put out. I was hoping he'd get the idea that I didn't really want to talk.

"Logan? Interesting. My friend Jacob has a dog named Logan. He's seven. Logan not Jacob. Do you have any pets?"

"I have a little brother. He's been house broke for a few years now."

"I have an older sister," said Alexander, barely letting me get the words out. "Her name is Alexis. And I have a younger sister, Allison."

The fixation on the letter "A" in Alexander's house continued with a dog named Adam and a lizard named Alli, "short for Alligator." I was soon longing for "Grandma Delores's" snoring.

"Did you see the last robot movie?"

"No," I said, even though the truth was I had, but I really didn't want to talk. I pulled a magazine and my

MP3 player out of my backpack. I hoped Alexander would get the drift and be quiet.

"Whoa! A surfer magazine. Do you surf?"

"I was born to surf." The response was out of my mouth before I could bring it back. It was something I'd said all my life. Something I'd believed until John Michael shot off his mouth. Born to surf, hah. Apparently, I was born to grow wheat or sunflowers or whatever it is people do for fun in Kansas. A shiver rocked my body as I thought of it. Alexander was still staring at me. "Nah, I'm just kidding you. I picked up the magazine at the bus station. I just wanted to look at the pictures."

"Sure. Anyway, in this movie there's this guy and he has this really cool gun. It's not like a normal gun because it has to kill the robots. But it doesn't really kill the robots because they're not really living, but it stops them. . . "

I nodded my head on occasion and slipped in a few "Yeahs" and "Wows" during the rare times he took a breath. The kid talked faster than the guys at the state fair trying to get you to waste twenty dollars for a two-dollar bear.

"The best part was when the guy busted down the door . . . "

The best part for me was yet to come because Alexander was still talking. It didn't take this long to watch the movie the first time. Dayton wouldn't take this long to retell a movie. Odd how I now missed the little pain-in-my-neck.

By now I had to assume he'd spilled all the information he had, and that David and Jill had found Rachel and realized I'd lied yet again. It wouldn't take long for them to find the checks and figure I'd run away. Hopefully, they'd be looking for a boy traveling alone to Kansas, not some boy traveling with his grandmother and a long-winded sidekick to Arkansas.

"Then at the end when you think they're all done this guy comes around the corner . . . "

Good he was reaching the end, maybe I was going to catch a break. "Hey great story, but I should check on my grandma."

Alexander craned his neck around the seats. "She's sleeping. Hey, you want to hear about this other movie I saw?"

"That'd be great," I said as I slumped back into the seat and leaned my head against the glass. The lower part of the window was dirty and made the countryside seem even more dull and boring. Between the vibrations on my head and the droning of Alexander's story in my ear, I was soon fast asleep.

CHAPTER 10

I'm not sure how long I slept but when I opened my eyes it was dark outside, and Alexander was finally quiet.

Reading lights created a faint yellow glow on the bus.

The sky looked like a giant Light Bright as the stars sparkled white, yellow, red, and blue against the black velvet canvas.

The ground, what I could see of it, looked like the moon, empty and cold. I couldn't imagine anyone living out there, and since I didn't see any streetlights, I assumed no one did.

The first highway sign in a long time came into view. The next major city was Flagstaff, Arizona. It was still hours away. However, it was now closer than home. I was no longer in California. It was fitting since I was no longer a Californian.

The bus jerked as it hit a bump, and my head smacked against the window.

"What was that?"

To my major disappointment the jostle woke Alexander.

"A rabbit. Go back to sleep," I said, rubbing my forehead.

"A rabbit," Alexander nearly yelled. "That must have been one big rabbit to shake the bus."

"Keep it down. It was probably a pothole."

"There was this one movie where a bus ran over a person and just kept going and then the person haunted the bus," Alexander said, becoming more animated with each word. "Maybe we ran over someone."

Strange how he wasn't as shook up about hitting a person as he was a rabbit. I closed my eyes and pictured the bus running over Alexander. Even in my thoughts, he just continued to talk about movies. He was like being haunted by a ghost, only not as fun.

I squirmed in my seat, trying to find a comfortable position. My legs didn't quite seem to fit anywhere. I had grown out of two pairs of shoes over the summer. The best was outgrowing a pair of dress pants before I even wore them. Jill bought them for some fancy family dinner. By the time we got around to going, the pants were three fingers above my ankle. Dayton will probably wear them to my funeral.

The bus hit another hole.

"Guess we ran over that guy again," Alexander said. "You think he'd learn."

"Dude, so true," I said. Maybe the movie critic wasn't so bad, he'd finally made me laugh. "Alex, you're okay."

"Thanks, Logan. Are you switching busses in Flagstaff?"

I hadn't looked at my ticket since getting on the bus. I wasn't sure of the actual route and figured the warden would just continue to tell me when and where to get off.

"I don't know. Do you?"

"Yeah, we're heading down to Phoenix. I was hoping to go to the Grand Canyon, but not this time."

The Grand Canyon. I'd seen pictures of it, read about, and studied it in geology, I didn't realize I'd be so close to it. I could take a little detour and do a little sightseeing.

It would probably mean traveling on without "Grandma Delores," but I'm sure I can handle it.

CHAPTER 11

The Flagstaff bus station was much smaller than the one in Los Angeles, but it was twice as busy. People meandering around the lobby trying to get tickets north to the Grand Canyon, others scurrying to catch their busses to Phoenix and points beyond.

"Bye, Logan," Alex called as his parents whisked him and the luggage toward another bus.

I was in no hurry to get back on another bus. My legs were having trouble remembering how to walk. I found information on travel to the Grand Canyon and would be able to re-route myself without losing any time. In fact, heading north would actually put me back on track to get to Fort Scott, Kansas.

The ticket-sales lady peered down her slim noise at me. "You're traveling alone?"

"No, I'm with my grandma."

"Then don't you want two tickets," she said as she counted the money I'd placed on the counter.

The idea of buying a ticket for someone who wasn't really my grandmother and who wasn't really going with me caused my stomach to turn. I hadn't thought of the added expense. However, the idea of seeing the Grand Canyon and not eating every meal was more appealing than traveling on and listening to Delores' snoring.

"Sorry, forgot," I said as I counted out the money for another ticket. I stuck the tickets into my pack and headed toward the door. It was time for some fresh air.

"Logan. Logan, where are you going?"

I turned to see "Grandma" shuffling toward me.

"Out to get some air."

"Don't go far our bus leaves soon," she said.

"I'm switching buses," I said, and tears started to form in her eyes. "I called my parents and my uncle is camping at the Grand Canyon, and they said I could go see him. It should be cool. I've never seen the Grand Canyon."

"That will be nice for you and him, but it will not be as enjoyable for me the rest of the trip."

"I'm sure you'll meet some other nice people."

"Maybe," she said and took a deep breath. "But you just remind me so much of my Billy. I lost him when he was about your age."

She reached out and touched my hair. I peeked to see if anyone was looking and was relieved that apparently no one else was witnessing this display of affection.

"He had an adventurous spirit," she continued. "He'd beg me to go off exploring, and I couldn't deny him. He reminded me of myself. That's what children do, you know. I'm sure your mom can't wait to be reunited with you."

My mom. Actually, it was my mom's. One I had run away from, the other had run away from me. Seemed I was closer to her than I could imagine. We were both runners. Technically, I was running toward something more than running from it. Either way, right now, I was motherless.

"Yeah, sure," I said. "I gotta run."

I didn't have time to stand around talking about moms and missing children, there was exploring to do.

The air and atmosphere in Flagstaff were flat compared to California. The idea of getting back on the bus was actually appealing.

I wandered back to the bus station and found the bus headed to the canyon. I tried to sell my other ticket, but no one wanted it even at half price.

I slipped in a seat about halfway back on the opposite side as the driver. Warden Bob was apparently headed for Phoenix. Warden Jack was my new controller.

I unfolded the informational map on the Grand Canyon to figure out where to go and what to do. I was going to have to be quick. The bus had two scheduled stops of an hour each on the south rim and then it was off to Colorado.

The scenery didn't really change much on the way to the canyon. The desert stretched for miles. Off in the distance rocks sprouted out of nowhere, but nothing prepared me for what I was about to see.

Pine trees blocked a clear view as the bus pulled into the parking lot near the visitor's center. The door on the bus opened and people stood in unison. After waiting my turn to merge into the aisle, I was finally off the bus and running in the direction everyone was pointing.

I skidded to a stop as my tennis shoes kicked up red dust. I lost my breath, but not because of the thinning air but because of the sight before me. There was a sunset frozen in the walls of the Grand Canyon.

Next to the ocean it was the biggest thing I'd ever seen. I slowly crept up to the edge and looked down and down and down. I saw several little birds below and watched them slowly rise on the air currents to realize they were actually very large raptors. They rode the wind like I rode waves, effortlessly, joyously. I imagined myself soaring with them, diving down the steep banks, skimming along the rushing Colorado River as it snaked through the bottom of the canyon.

My flight of fancy was disturbed by kids playing keep-away with someone's shoe. Their laughter was joined by the loud voices of parents arguing about where to go for dinner and if their kids really needed two shoes each.

Next to them was a group of people from Korea. I didn't understand what they were saying, but I did recognize the flag on their sleeves. I guessed they were just as annoyed by the game of keep-away as I was, and I wished I could say it without others understanding me.

Too soon it was time to get back on the bus and head off to the desert view and watch tower. It was a great area for exploring. I flew up the stairs of the tower, passing people who were too winded to make it to the top of the winding staircase. The view from the top was amazing.

On the first floor, members of the Navajo Nation were making a rug and others were selling homemade jewelry. I bought a leather necklace with a bear carved out of stone for Dayton and one with a stone turtle for Blue. I just wasn't sure when I could give it to them.

CHAPTER 12

"There you are young man."

I whirled around at the sound of the voice. "Mom?"

The lady shot a quick glance at me and walked past me to a boy who was climbing a fence on the edge of the canyon.

Between Delores' story of Billy, buying things for Dayton, and the lady's voice, I was starting to feel slightly guilty for running away. Not too guilty, just a bit. After all, I was the one who was adopted. I was the one who had been lied to all these years.

Then why did I wish for a second that the lady had been my mom? No, she was Jill now. There was just one thing to do.

I looked around and found a pay phone. I got several dollars' worth of change from the gift shop, since I wasn't sure how much this was going to cost me. I could have called collect if I'd called home, but I wasn't feeling that guilty.

"Hello, Driftwood Complex."

"Hi. Is Blue there?"

"Let me check."

I could hear the man asking if people had seen Blue, asking them to find him because he had a phone call.

"He's coming. Who is this?"

"A traveler."

"Cool. Here he is."

"Hey," said Blue in a voice that made me even more homesick.

"Blue, it's me, Logan."

"Dude, where are you?"

"*Shhhh*," I said afraid people between here and California had heard him.

"Sorry, bud," he said in a whisper. "Where are you?"

"I don't want to tell you, so you won't have to lie if people ask you if you've heard from me."

"Thanks for looking out for me. What you been up to?"

"Let's just say I'm on the adventure of a lifetime. However, it would be a more-excellent adventure if you and Dayton were with me. I've seen some amazing plants and animals."

"Please, deposit another twenty-five cents," the recorded voice cut in. I grabbed a quarter and dropped it in the slot.

"You still there, Blue?"

"Yeah. Dude, I wish I was with you, too. Things are crazy around here. Your parents . . . "

"They're not my parents," I broke in.

"Whatever. Your parents nearly died when they found the open envelopes and the checks. They looked like they were going to faint. Your mom . . . "

"Jill."

"Whatever. Your mom was whiter than Dayton's hair when he bleached it last summer."

"Whoa, that's pretty white," I laughed at the memory of my brother's experiment gone wrong.

"Are you okay?" Blue asked quietly.

"I'm not sure." Which was pretty close to the truth for me. "I'm starting to run low on money, but I've been eating. I haven't been getting any good sleep, but I've met some interesting people. I even got you and Dayton a gift."

"Cool. What is it?"

"You'll have to wait and see. How is Dayton doing?"

"Please, deposit another twenty-five cents." I reached for a quarter and knocked the change off the ledge.

"Oh, no," I scrambled to pick up the coins. I could faintly hear the voice asking for more money. "Give me a second." As soon as I'd picked up a coin, it squirted out of my hand. "I just need one. Got it."

I put the receiver back to my ear and only heard buzzing.

It was followed by the now familiar *fa-woosh* sound of the bus door closing. "Oh, no, the bus."

Leaving several dollars' worth of change on the ground, I took off running. The bus was headed my way, and I waved my arms as I ran toward it. The driver and I made eye contact. I'd seen that look. It was not a good one. I was thankful he slowed and let me get on the bus. The look told me he wanted to speed up and have me ride on the front bumper the rest of the trip.

"Thanks," I said, quickly slipping past him to find a seat. Unfortunately for me, the only seats available were behind Warden Jack. It was going to be a long ride as he stared me down every time he glanced in the rear-view mirror. A very long ride.

The lady next to me was reading some gardening magazines. She nearly read aloud, a few words here and there were audible. I wanted to tell her, either read all the way out loud or keep your lips from moving. But since the warden was already mad at me, it didn't seem prudent to get everyone upset with me. I pulled out my magazines and started reading. It was fun to mimic the lady and say every fourth and sixth word out loud. She just kept right on mumbling, but the soldier across the aisle knocked me on the elbow.

"Hey, kid. Read to yourself."

The name embroidered on his camouflage shirt was Carson. He had a Ranger patch on his shoulder and was wearing skater shoes. He wasn't your average soldier.

"What outfit are you with?"

"*Huh?*"

"You're in the Army, right?"

"Are you kidding me? I just picked this up at a thrift store."

"So, you're not in the Army? Why wear the shirt?"

"It looks cool on me."

I didn't want to tell him it was the shoes that were cool not the shirt. I turned back to my magazine. There was an ad for the surfboard I was going to get. I traced its outline and tried to recall the smell and feel of the ocean. My senses weren't quite as sharp, but I could still hear the roaring of the waves.

"I miss you my blue friend."

Instead of sitting on a freshly waxed board waiting to catch the next wave, I'm sitting in a ratty old bus on a seat with a busted spring that pokes me in the butt every time we hit a bump. Worse yet, this was a very bumpy road. I wiggled in the seat to try and get comfortable. I must have bumped the lady.

"Where is your mother?" she said looking around.

"At home."

"Your father on this bus?"

"No," I said.

The lady's eyes got big. She kept glancing front and back faster and faster as if that would make my parents appear on the bus.

"You're on this bus alone?"

"No." It wasn't a lie because there were other people on the bus.

"Who are you with? I'm going to tell the bus driver to put you together."

"No," I said grabbing her arm. I didn't want the warden having anymore contact with me. I didn't want people having too many memories in case Jill and David started calling around. "I'm with my brother." I said as I reached over and patted the pseudo-soldier's arm.

"Is he your brother?" she asked him.

I locked my eyes on him, nodding with as little movement as possible. Maybe he read my mind. Maybe he was a pathological liar like me. For whatever reason, he saved me.

"Are you bothering the lady, Nimrod?" he said and popped me on the side of my head.

"*Ouch.*"

She quieted down and went back to her book.

I leaned across the aisle. "I'd never hurt my brother."

"Me neither," he whispered, "but you're *not* my brother."

Ah, but I could be. Yuck, what a terrible thought. I missed Dayton.

CHAPTER 13

I'm not sure where I am any more.

The canyon lands are one massive blend of colored rock. I pick out one red monolith to judge distance and another one pops up in its place farther down the road. It's as if the scenery were on a giant conveyor belt that just keeps spinning the same view around and around and around and around.

Carson the faux soldier moved to the front of the bus to sit next to a girl. I saw her earlier. She's hard to miss with the silver link chain from her ear to her nose. I wasn't sure why he wanted to sit with her. I wasn't sure why boys sat with girls. I liked sitting with Sally, but she was an awesome surfer and, so not really a girl.

There was only so much time in a day, and I'd rather figure out how to get in a full day of riding waves and skateboarding than talking to most girls. Of course, it did get Carson the fake soldier out of arm's reach of me for a while. Maybe girls aren't such a bad thing.

With him out of the way, I could now see the lady across the aisle. She was holding a baby with one arm and a basic math book in her free hand. She wore a UCLA T-shirt. All I could see was the "A," but anyone with half-a-brain would recognize the baby-blue and gold coloring.

The baby started to cry, and she bounced the blue bundle. The crying started to get louder.

"Jill would sing to make Dayton quiet."

"Excuse me," she said, looking at me and putting down the book to use both arms to try and quiet the baby.

"Dayton, my little brother, would cry, and Jill would sing to him."

"Who's Jill?"

"She used to be my mom."

"I'm sorry for your loss," she said. "Want to come sit here?"

The gardening lady was still looking at her magazines, so taking a quick peek to make sure the warden wasn't looking, I slipped across the aisle. I picked up the book and put it on my lap.

"I didn't lose her," I said, flipping over the book. "This a college book? Looks easy."

"It's an introductory class," she took the book from me and put it down in her bag. "What do you mean you didn't lose your mom?"

I'd already said too much. Her blonde hair, blue eyes and Southern California tan held me in some sort of spell. It was time for evasive measures.

"What's the baby's name?"

"Joshua. Where's your mom?"

"That's a nice name. She's at home. Is he named after his dad? How old is he? Joshua, not his dad."

"Thanks. He's six weeks. He looks like his dad," she said as she pulled back the blanket from near his face. He looked round and plain like most babies I'd seen. Dayton was different because he had white hair.

"He's cute." It was probably the longest I'd gone in a conversation before telling a lie. I'm not even sure if it was a lie. For all I know the baby was cute. "Kind of little for taking a bus trip isn't he?"

"Same could be said for you."

She was good.

"I'm thirteen, and I have family at the end of the line."

"Us, too."

"Cool. Where are you getting off?"

"Denver. We're going to stay with my parents."

"Bet they're happy to be grandparents and to see Joshua."

Her face turned pale, like Blue's after riding a roller-coaster. She looked down at the baby. She caressed his cheek, and he stopped fussing and smiled back. "No one is really thrilled when their unmarried baby comes home with a baby."

"I'm sorry. I didn't know." I looked down at the floor and watched my feet tap.

"It's okay. I'm not sure why I'm telling you this," she said between sniffles.

I didn't want to look at her and see her crying. I didn't want to embarrass her, but apparently, I had some magic pull on her also. Two Southern Californians on a bus headed for uncertain futures.

"What's your name?"

"Logan."

"Hi, Logan. I'm Katie."

I saw her hand come across the seat and I shook it. I looked at her and smiled. She returned the smile and brushed away tears from her cheek.

"It hurts to leave, huh?"

"It's not that easy going home."

"You're not from California?"

"No. I'm from Colorado. Don't let the hair—colored—and tan—from a bottle—fool you," she said with a wink and reached out and tried to fix my hair.

"Hey," I said pushing her hand away, "it's taken several hours on a bus to get this look."

We laughed, and it even sounded like Joshua tried to join us. Unfortunately, his giggle soon turned to crying. Katie tried bouncing, singing, and rocking. Nothing worked. Her face tightened and tears were on the verge of spilling.

"Why don't you let me hold him? Jill let me hold Dayton."

She passed the squirming blanket to me, and I pulled him close like Jill had told me: "Babies need to feel safe and loved." It usually worked. I hummed any lullaby that came into my mind, the one about twinkling stars, twice. Slowly Joshua stopped crying and was soon asleep.

"You're a kid, and you're better at this than me," Katie said, turning toward the window. "Maybe I should have given him to that family."

"What?" I wasn't sure if I'd heard her right. "You were going to give your baby away? Why?"

"Keep your voice down. I don't want everybody knowing my business. I thought about it, but I couldn't."

"What did you think about?"

"You ask a lot of questions."

"Just a curious kid, I guess," I said, looking down at Joshua, who was sucking on his hand. "He must be dreaming he's eating. You're glad you kept him, right?"

"Ask me that in eighteen years, or better yet, eighteen months or eighteen hours."

I was extremely confused. Jill and David were thrilled to bring Dayton home. They were excited about a family. But Katie seemed to dread the idea.

"Logan, things get complicated when you get older."

"My life is already pretty complicated."

"I had my whole life planned out: college, career, family. Not to put off college and a career for a family. I'd been dating Joshua's dad for a year. When he found out I was pregnant, he said to get rid of the baby. I couldn't. I thought about giving him up for adoption, but my parents said they'd help. But only if I came home. So, I'm on my way home."

Maybe my real grandparents weren't willing to help my real mom. Maybe she never asked them. Maybe her boyfriend was much more persuasive. I now had some

TO WHOM IT MAY CONCERN:

possible answers to one side of the story. I was no closer
to finding out why Jill and David lied, but I was closer
to the end of the line.

CHAPTER 14

Growing up in California, I was convinced everything great was in the Golden State. This cross-country bus trip was slowly changing my mind.

The Grand Canyon was amazing and now climbing through the Rocky Mountains made the southern Sierra Nevada range seem like a bump in the road. We climbed higher and higher. My ears started to hurt. Joshua's must have, too, because he was extra fussy. I couldn't see him because Carson the thrift-store soldier had returned and shoved me out of the seat.

Apparently, the girl up front was no longer interesting. I'm not sure what happened, all I know is he stomped back, lifted me out of the seat by my shirt and tossed me across the aisle. All the while mumbling "stupid vegetarians," "get out of my seat," and "can't wait to get off this dumb bus." I agreed with the last part.

I tried swallowing hard to pop my ears. It worked when we'd gone skiing at Big Bear. I also tried yawning, but that caused the gardening lady to ask me if I was tired.

"No, my ears are plugged."

"Want some gum?"

So, I was now chewing gum, still waiting for them to pop. I was nearly desperate to grab my nose and blow to relieve the pressure. However, I remembered that Dayton said he heard from Bob Myers who heard from a doctor on TV that doing that could cause serious ear damage. I was willing to take the chance for some relief when we hit the top of the pass and started down. On the third switchback, my ears popped on their own, and once again I could hear clearly. Which was bad because Joshua was still crying. If only he could chew gum.

The mountains brought new scenery that was greatly needed. Now instead of everything being earth tones, everything was green. Trees sprouted nearly everywhere, and where there weren't trees there were green bushes or green grasses. Even after the longest California rainstorms, I'd never seen that much green at once. I didn't know there was that much green to be seen.

And rivers rushing with water. Water was nearly as plentiful as the trees. Creeks ran down the mountainside and collided with the river below. Aside from the ocean, to see other water at home took a ride to the aqueduct. The Los Angeles River usually trickled down the middle of its concrete banks.

Even the little towns where we stopped were more exciting in Colorado. Maybe it was just the cool mountain air that made them friendly. Whatever it was, it was a nice break from the desert doldrums.

We finally made a pit stop. I used the stop to get off and find a restroom. I wasn't sure how much longer I could go without using the one on the bus, but the smells that hit me ten rows from the toilet were enough to keep me in my seat until we hit a town.

On my way back to the bus, I grabbed a pack of gum and a disposable camera. I didn't know how many more mountains there were or how long the lady would continue giving me gum.

In addition, I decided to document my journey. After all, aside from Blue and Dayton, who would believe my story if I didn't have proof? They'd have to take my word for "Grandma Delores" and Alex, but from now on, everyone and everything would be catalogued.

The warden growled when I took his picture as I got on the bus, seemed fitting. The chain girl smiled, the gardening lady looked down at her magazine, the soldier put his hand up, and Katie pulled back the blanket from Joshua's face.

Joshua finally found relief and was enjoying a bottle. Katie let me hold him, so I could have a picture of us together.

"Here kid you sit with the baby," my fake big brother said getting up and changing places with me.

"Thanks, Carson."

"Thom. My name is Thom."

"Thanks, Thom."

It was nice to be next to Katie and Joshua. She was comfortable to sit with for a girl with a baby.

"Katie are we almost there?"

"Not much longer now," she said and repeated quieter. "Not much longer."

"Is there anything to do in Denver that could be fun?"

"You won't have that long before your next bus. You'll have to come back some time with your family."

"Which one," I said under my breath.

"What's that?"

"Katie, can I tell you something, but you have to swear on Joshua's life that you won't tell a soul. Promise."

"Sounds serious," she said with a slight smile.

"Promise me."

"Okay, Logan, I promise."

I leaned in really close to her ear. She started to pull back. I placed my hand on her head, so she couldn't move anymore.

"I'm adopted."

She looked at me and tilted her head in that "and" way.

"And . . . I'm on my way to find my real mother and father."

"Logan, you've run away from home?"

"*Shhhhhh*," I said, quickly glancing around to see who was now paying attention to the conversation. "I'm running home."

"Why would you want to leave home?"

"Jill and David lied to me."

"Who are Jill and David?"

"My parents. Well, the people who've been raising me," I adjusted. "But they lied. They're hiding something from me, but I don't know what. I'm going to find my birth parents and the truth."

"Do they know you're coming?"

"Who?"

"Your birth parents. Did you contact people and make arrangements?"

It hit me like a wave breaking early and pummeling me into the sand. I hadn't even thought about how to find them. I hadn't thought about "arrangements" and "contacts."

"Yeah, it's all set," I said, hoping my face wouldn't give away the truth. "In fact, they seem very excited to see me."

"That's great," Katie said, but her face didn't agree with her words. She knew I was lying. Joshua started to cry, and I reached to find a pacifier only to realize he wasn't the one crying. The soft sobbing was coming from the seat in front of Katie. I could barely see the person through the space between the seats. I was tempted to stand on my seat and find out what they were doing that was making them cry, but I decided it would draw the warden's attention.

Denver was not much farther and with any luck I'd get a new warden, maybe one that I could actually call by the name on their shirt.

The bus came around a corner and the view out the window showed a vast expanse of flatness on the horizon. There near where the mountains faded into the plains sprawled a massive metropolis with a hazy brown cloud that rivaled Los Angeles.

"There it is Logan. Denver."

CHAPTER 15

enver was a nice break from the little towns. The massive high-rise buildings were dwarfed by the Rocky Mountains, but it was at least a real-size city. It even had traffic jams.

The bus sat trapped in gridlock on the freeway. It idled hard and rattled like a massage chair with a busted coil. I was very glad I took the opportunity to empty my bladder at the last stop. All the shaking may have forced me to use the dreaded traveling facilities.

Joshua was pulling at Katie's hair, but she kept her face toward the window. He started to squirm in her arms, but she didn't look at him.

"He's excited about being here," I said to the back of Katie's head.

She nodded and breathed an "*ah-huh*" without looking at me. I didn't understand Katie's situation, but I knew mine. I wasn't in any big hurry to see my parents either.

The bus finally started moving again and was able to get off the freeway. It was time to get ready to switch busses and head further into the unknown.

"Would you like some help getting everything together?" I said, folding one of Joshua's blankets.

She turned and took the blanket and stuffed it in the diaper bag. She half-smiled and mouthed "thank you." Joshua giggled and wiggled some more. She pulled him close. "We'll be okay, Logan. You take care of yourself."

I doubled-checked under my seat for magazines, tunes, and snacks. I even slipped under Thom's feet to make sure I didn't leave anything across the aisle.

"You're one weird kid," he said, as he smiled and lifted his feet.

"Thanks," I said, as much for his moving his feet to the back-handed compliment.

I could see the bus depot now. I always liked to be ready, so as soon as the bus stopped, I could be up and out. I was usually one of the first people off and avoided standing and waiting for the other people to get their stuff together. Others must have been thinking the same thing because it was like synchronized seat evacuation as most of the people stood as one giant wave.

TO WHOM IT MAY CONCERN:

I was sandwiched between Thom and a tall man from two rows up. Unable to move anywhere or see anything in front of me, I glanced to see who was sitting in front of Katie. Turns out an older lady—probably in her thirties—was the one who had been crying. She glanced at me, and I showed off my pearly whites. She tried to return the favor, but it looked more like a squiggle than a smile.

I looked forward and was greeted with the back of the tall man. I leaned left and right to try and see who was causing the hold up. The man turned out to be as wide as he was tall.

The odd feeling that comes from being stared at started to creep up on me. I half-glanced at the lady and her eyes were locked on me. I nodded and smiled again. She didn't respond. She just stared, almost like she was looking through me instead of at me. Before I could ask her what she was staring at, Thom pushed me.

"Keep the line moving."

I twisted to look at him. "Don't get pushy."

He shook his head and patted my shoulder. "Move it, Little Brother," he said with a wink.

I headed for the exit, saying a quick goodbye to the warden on my way out. Free at last, or at least until the next bus.

Until then, I needed to find a phone. There was no answer at Blue's house. It would have been great to hear Dayton's voice but knowing Jill and David they would have been keeping quiet around him. I needed answers. I called the one person who always told me the truth and would be willing to take a collect call.

"Hello."

"Rachel? Rachel, it's me, Logan."

"Yes, the operator told me, dear. Logan, where are you? Your parents are sick with worry. We're all worried about you."

"Sick with worry" that was a good sign. It was better than hearing they'd put a "For Rent" sign on my bedroom door.

"I'm okay. Did they tell you anything? Do you know?"

"Did they tell me you're adopted? Yes. But why runaway?"

"They're hiding something from me. There has to be some big secret otherwise they would have told me. Mom almost rubbed the skin off her hands. It must be something big, like I'm a secret experiment. Remember the movie where the kid wasn't a kid but a robot? Maybe I'm a robot."

"Logan, listen to yourself. Your parents love you. Yes, they could have told you sooner. But you shouldn't have run away. Running never solved anything. Are you sure it's your parents you're angry with?"

"What do you mean? Who else would I be mad at?"

"The young lady who left you. You for not being who you thought you were, or your cousin for telling you. Seems like you have a lot of people to be angry with."

"I'm adopted. I'm nobody's. Do you know what that's like?"

"Yes."

I didn't expect that. "You're adopted, Rachel?"

"I was a nobody until I was adopted into the biggest family of all—by God. He makes us one big family with Jesus as our big brother."

"It's not the same. You knew you were adopted. God didn't keep any secrets."

"True, but being adopted is so special. You were chosen by your parents. Chosen, Logan, do you understand? They could have decided to leave you alone in the world. God could have left us alone, but He didn't. He chose us. He chose to love us, to take us in, to create for us a home."

Rachel's words were like a riptide in my heart, creating a vacuum that gets back filled and takes everything out with it. You can't fight it. You have to go with it. I didn't want to go with it, and the only way to fight it was to hang up. It was a cowardly way of dealing with the situation, but it was also the fastest.

"Rachel, I have to go. Tell Jill and David I'm okay."

"I will tell *your parents* that you love them. Logan, I'm praying for you."

"Thanks." I knew she'd actually been praying since she'd heard. By now all the people at her church knew, and they'd be praying, too. I wasn't much of a praying person. Oh, I'd asked for good weather and a puppy along the way, but I'm thinking that's more wishing than praying.

My prayer now was to find my real mother and what Jill and David were hiding. I didn't really think I was a robot, but I wasn't feeling much like a human either.

CHAPTER 16

Why didn't I fly? It would have been so much faster.

Of course, I knew the answer was because I didn't have the money. I also knew that I'd never take a long bus ride anywhere again.

I also never wanted to eat fast food again. I craved a home-cooked meal. Jill's enchiladas were my favorite, along with cheese pizza. I would have eaten both had I stuck around for my birthday lunch. Now, I was three states away and hungry.

My lack of money-management skills finally caught up with me. I had bought two bus tickets all along the way even though I'd traveled the last several hundred miles by myself. Between extra tickets and snacks, my wallet was starting to look like a black hole—nothing was coming out of it.

According to the schedule, I should be in Fort Scott by the next morning. My ticket there was paid for, but I only had twenty dollars left for everything else. Food may become a special treat.

Although I wouldn't be able to buy Dayton or Blue any more gifts, I decided to explore the station and its surroundings. I lost track of the familiar faces from my last ride. My insides started to do flip-flops when I realized I was alone in a strange city. My stomach began to quiet as I stepped outside and breathed some "fresh" air. Just as I breathed deeply, a bus pulled out and belched exhaust. It nearly made me gag.

A group of boys were grinding the rails with their skateboards at the far end of the block. I headed for them, passing several "No skateboarding allowed on sidewalks" signs. It wasn't surfing, but even I took a turn on four wheels when the waves quieted down.

The biggest boy hoisted up his pants between kick flips and ollies. A freckle-faced kid tried to follow but lost his footing and ended up on his butt. The other boys started to laugh as he stood up slowly and rubbed his bottom.

"Can I try?" I asked Freckles. I figured he wouldn't be in too big of a hurry to get back on the rail.

"You know how?" he asked, scanning my clothes, and focusing on my shoes. I had the newest Vans at home, but I didn't pack them. Last year's high-tops covered my size-10 feet.

"I can't do any worse than you." The pack of boys started to laugh again. I felt bad that Freckles seemed to be the source of the group's laughter. "Come, on, Dude," I said. "Just one ride."

"'Dude?' Man, you aren't from around here," said the big boy, whose pants continued to sag near his knees. "What bus did you get off?"

"I'm from California."

"Give him your board, Red."

I wasn't sure Red was the boy's name any more than Freckles, but he handed me the skateboard. I hopped on and checked out the balance. The wheels were fatter than the ones on my board and the balance seemed off, but a wobbly ride is better than no ride at all. I started with a standard ollie. No need in giving away all my tricks in the first run.

"Show him something, Jas." The group called to the big boy. He jumped on the bench and tried to kick flip to a higher railing that guarded a set of five stairs. He was an inch short and bounced back. He was fast enough to grab the top rail and keep from falling down the stairs.

I let him get out of the way and then started the same trick. I heard the group say, "Oh, no," and guessed they were worried I would suffer the same fate as Jas. What I didn't figure was seeing a shiny badge as I landed on the rail. There was another officer waiting at the bottom of the stairs. He grabbed me and the board rolled free across the parking lot.

"My board," Red said as his face turned the same color as his hair.

"Forget it and run," Jas said. The group scattered and I was left alone in the custody of Denver's finest.

"Can't you read, boy?" said the tall police officer. "Go get your board."

"It's not mine. I was just borrowing it." I wasn't going to address whether or not I could read. "I'm just waiting for a bus."

"Well, we'll return you to your parents." The other officer, Wilson, according to his badge, grabbed me under the arm and pulled me up to walk on my tiptoes. It was a good thing my parents weren't there because they would have been embarrassed. Half-walking, half-being-dragged by Wilson, I stumbled into the station.

"Where are your parents?"

"I don't see them."

"We'll put you in the office and page them."

"That's not necessary, Officer. I've learned my lesson. Really."

"Sit down there," he said as he pushed me in the direction of a green chair that had started to spit out its stuffing. "What's your name? And your parents' names?"

Before I could answer his question, there was a knock at the door. The tall officer came in with my backpack and started whispering. I strained to hear and made out "his mother" and "ran away." Jill was here in Denver?

"Your mother's coming. Apparently, she saw you being hauled in. Bryant said she's not looking too pleased."

The door opened and I prepared myself to face Jill, to hear her voice rip me for my bad behavior, to smell her perfume, and to go home.

The crying lady walked through the door.

"Robert Raymond Richardson, you should be ashamed."

I was speechless. It wasn't my mother. It wasn't even my name. But the officer was buying it, and it was getting me out of trouble. She came over and latched onto my ear and pulled me up from the chair with one hand and snatched my backpack with the other. Jill never pulled my ear.

"You are in big trouble, young man. Wait until we meet up with your grandfather." She was doing a great job of acting. I was actually starting to be afraid.

Once I thought we were far enough away from the police, I tried to pull away. She tightened her grip.

"Hey, lady, thanks for the help. Now, let me go."

"That is no way to talk to your mother, young man. Keep up. We nearly missed our bus."

Our bus?

"My bus is headed for Fort Scott and doesn't leave for another hour. Can I, please, have my backpack?"

"Don't talk back, Robert. I'm still very angry with you for your behavior. I'll be keeping your things while you think about what you've done."

"My name is Logan. Logan Fisher." I tried to pry her vice lock off my ear, but the more I tried the tighter she squeezed. My ear was a mouse caught in her boa-like grip. Walking faster and taller relieved some of the pressure.

TO WHOM IT MAY CONCERN:

I saw Bus 52 with its glowing sign board, which included Fort Scott. Was she going to make us sit on the bus for hours? As if things couldn't get worse, I saw Warden Bob behind the wheel. He seemed to smile when he saw me walking toward him under the control of an adult. I could not return the smile. I started to turn to get in the door when the lady jerked my ear.

"Ouch," I said, grabbing my ear and her hand. "That's my bus."

She didn't say anything. She increased the pace. I looked back at Bus 52 and the Warden. I'm not quite sure, but I thought I saw him frown. I knew I was frowning.

"Here's our bus," she said, shoving me up the stairs. The circulation started to return to my ear. "I'm sorry for the delay," she said to the bus driver. She pushed me into a seat. I couldn't catch myself in time and my sore ear collided with the window.

I wanted to scream that I was being kidnapped. But can a kid who's running away really be kidnapped or was I being hijacked? I'd just wait for an opportunity and make a break for it. I was going to need to keep my wits about me.

"Where are we going?"

"I don't like your tone. I'm so ashamed."

The crying lady had that vacant look like people in the zombie movies. Either someone had sucked out her brain or she was going to try and suck out mine. Maybe I was an alien and not a robot, maybe she was taking me back to the home planet. No, that was just stupid.

It was time for some crafty talking.

"I'm very sorry, Mother. Please forgive my horrible behavior."

"Oh, how can I stay mad at you?" she said, grabbing me on the shoulders and pulling me in close for a hug. "Your grandfather is going to be so surprised to see you."

"Surprised?"

"Happy. I mean happy," she said, running her fingers through my hair and pinching my cheeks. "I'm just so glad I found you. I'd started to think I was never going to find you."

"I just stepped outside."

"I told your grandfather that I'd find you. That nurse stole you, but I told him I'd find you." She pulled me close and grabbed my hands and started to count my fingers. "Oh, perfect, ten fingers. How perfect."

"I have ten toes, too."

"Of course you do, Robert. You're perfect. Just how I knew you'd be."

It was obvious the crying lady had made the leap to irrational lady. Somehow, she decided I was her long-lost son. I wiggled free and looked out the window. The road sign gave the distance to Cheyenne. We were headed north toward Wyoming.

I needed to go east.

CHAPTER 17

C.B., it seemed nicer than continuing to call her the Crying Bus lady, kept one hand on me at all times.

She was either messing with my hair, recounting my fingers, or hugging my shoulders. I worried she'd want to start counting my toes soon.

She didn't seem to need sleep, which was not helping my planning. I needed her to not only fall asleep, but to stay asleep, when the bus stopped. Even then it wasn't going to be easy. I tried to pull away the few times she'd dozed off, but her hand was super-glued in place. So, I decided to work on a Plan B. I'm not sure it would be a true Plan B, since I never fully formulated a Plan A, but there was no time to worry about that now.

The one thing I knew was I had to get away at the first stop. I couldn't afford to go too far north. I needed to get back on track, and I needed to get away from C.B. ASAP.

Sitting close to the window, I created as much space as I could between myself and C.B. It still felt too close. It was like being a cricket in a chameleon's cage. Sure, you had freedom to move around, but at any minute that lightning-fast tongue could flick out and, slurp, you're done for. Yeah, this lady made life uneasy.

Eventually, the bus would stop. I had to be ready to create on the go and get away with my backpack, which had my money, Dayton's and Blue's gifts, and a bus ticket to Fort Scott.

The chameleon inched closer and touched my cheek.

"Once you're back home," she said calmly. "I'll have grandfather put locks on the outside of the door, so no one can take you away again."

"Are you crazy?" I asked a tad too loudly as she jerked back and shook her head.

"Don't call me that," she said, moving quickly back toward me. Our noses were separated by a thin sheet of air. "Don't you ever call me that again."

Her tone and expression sent a chill down my back and the hairs on my neck stood up.

"Sorry . . . Momma?"

"You're forgiven," the chameleon said, inching ever closer. "And call me, Mother."

I was now a cricket with a very large bullseye painted on it.

"Get some rest, Robert."

Oh, sure she wants me to sleep. She wants me to get relaxed, so it won't hurt as much when she eats me alive and spits me out in some prison room in some remote Midwest town. No, I would not sleep. I might be trapped, but I was still free.

I felt the bus starting to slow down. We passed a campground on the outskirts of town. The campground was full of campers, motorhomes, and a few tents.

"Robert, we'll get off, but you stay close."

All the bus stops started to feel the same. Small facilities near a gas station and a lot of fast-food chains.

"Are you hungry?"

I wasn't hungry, but a plan was coming together.

"Yeah. I'd like a double chili-cheese deluxe burger. Plus, large fries and a milk shake."

"That seems like a lot. Are you sure?"

I nodded and even tossed in the Mother-may-I sad eyes for good measure. It was overkill, but it worked.

"Oh, don't go looking at me like that."

I held out my hand hoping she'd give me the money, and I'd just make a run for it.

"Oh, no, you don't. We'll go together."

Darn.

It smelled of burnt cheese and too many chili eaters in the building. The stench stopped C.B. in her tracks.

"Oh, my goodness. This place is horrid."

"I can get it myself."

"No, no. I'm okay. Just be quick about it."

A kid a few years older than me took the order, and I had my lunch on the tray before he could give her the change.

"Let's eat in here by the window," I said.

"No, we'll eat outside."

We sat down on a bench under a tree. I realized we were on the side of the bus opposite the door. I had a Plan B.

I shoved as much of the burger into my mouth as I could. Chili and processed cheese oozed out and onto my cheeks. Some even found its way into my nose.

"Robert, stop it. Eat like a gentleman." C.B. pulled my hands down and wiped away the chili and cheese from around my mouth.

"Sawry, I'm ungry," I said attempting to swallow what was in my mouth. I chugged some milkshake and sawed through some fries, then it was back to the burger. I kept my eye on the bus driver and the passengers. The bus driver had already looked at his watch twice. If he was anything like the Warden, he'd look at it three times and pull out five minutes after the last look. I was hoping they were the same.

Look No. 3: Start the countdown. I shoveled in the rest of the burger, guzzled down the milkshake and shoved in the remaining fries. All the while, ignoring calls for proper manners.

After the last bite, I grabbed my stomach and started moaning.

"Oh, man, I need a bathroom."

"There's one at the gas station or in the restaurant," she said.

"No, they're too dirty," I said, hoping her need for cleanliness was as great as her need for manners.

"You're right. Go on the bus."

I choked and nearly lost my lunch. She must not be smelling the same bus I'm smelling, but it helped my plan.

"Okay," I said as I reached for my backpack next to her.

"No, I'll hold on to this."

I didn't want to overplay my hand and lose a chance
to get away. I decided getting away was more important
than the contents of my pack, so I ran to the bus holding my stomach. No one was on the bus but the driver.
I slunk by him head low, groaning. I glanced over to
see C.B. and half waved at her. I turned back to make
sure the bus driver saw me open the bathroom door. A
hundred dirty socks and fifty wet dogs smelled better
than this bathroom.

When the warden looked down, I quickly shut the
door and slipped into the aisle. I crawled on my hands
and knees up to the first seats. Like clockwork, he
honked the horn.

People started to file onto the bus. Guitar guy was
getting back on with his Fender. Between him and the
instrument, people were being bumped around and not
looking down. I stealthily slipped between the guitar
and the door. Staying low, I headed toward the back of
the bus.

C.B. would come to the front, she wouldn't want to
be near the exhaust. There was no one on the bench. I
ran straight back from the bus and hid behind a hedge
that divided the burger place from the taco stand. The
bus pulled away. It was the best sight of the day.

TO WHOM IT MAY CONCERN:

If all went well, C.B. would figure I was getting sick in the bathroom. This would work until someone else got up to use the bathroom or the chameleon's need for a cricket kicked in.

All I knew is she was going to need to find another snack.

CHAPTER 18

The queasy feeling in my stomach grew. I was either sick at the thought of being alone in a strange place or from gorging myself on chili. It wasn't the first time I'd been alone. It was the first time I was isolated. I was fine being alone in my room or out on the beach by myself for hours. That was because I knew exactly where Dayton and Blue were, and I could have company at any time. I still knew where they were, but I wasn't going to have either for company today.

With no follow-up plan, it was time to head back toward Denver. I hoped a plan would form on the way. I needed to find a place for the night since my traditional sleeping space was speeding away down the highway. Which brought up the fact, I needed to find a new ride to Fort Scott.

The sound hit my ears like the voice of a long-lost friend. The deep, throaty roar of a Harley-Davidson motorcycle. Bikers rode them up and down the

California coast all summer long. The sound shattered the Colorado quiet as the group flew past me, leaving me choking on the exhaust and kicked up dust. For the first time in a long time, it felt like home.

I lost sight of the motorcycles as they cruised down the highway, but I could hear them. I walked in the deep gully that ran next to the road to avoid being hit by cars and, more importantly, avoid being seen. The ditch was full of wildflowers and prairie grasses that slapped at my waist. The ground sloped up to meet an intersecting road. I was across from the campground. I had found the answer to my sleeping problem.

Wandering through the campground, I noticed several families setting up tents and preparing their cooking areas. With all the families, no one was going to take notice of one more kid running around.

Toward the back were several travel tents in a semicircle. No one was currently at home in any of them. The biggest tent had a storage box off the back. The box sat on a table about two feet off the ground. Sliding under the table, I noticed I could lift the protective skirt around the trailer just enough to slip under it. I took inventory of each of the tents. I borrowed a tarp from one, a blanket from one, a pillow from one, and a quilt from one. I crawled back under and proceeded to make my bed. I wasn't tired, but it needed to be ready, so I could just get in later.

With my lodging taken care of, it was time to explore. Before I got to the next group of campers, I heard the Harleys. The thunder grew as they pulled into the back section of the campground. There were some Honda Gold Wings in the group also, but I hadn't heard them. Nothing is heard over a Hog.

Wait until I tell Dayton and Blue about "borrowing" from Harley riders.

Most of the riders appeared to be Jill and David's age. David wanted a motorcycle, but Jill always said "No." Apparently, these guys' wives were more open-minded. They had to be, most of them had women with them. Women would ruin the trip for me, but they would be good for cooking and cleaning on the road.

I must have been staring too long because one of the bikers yelled in my direction and waved his arm for me to come over.

"You want a close-up look, kid?"

I glanced around to make sure he was talking to me.

"Yes, you."

"Sure." I had been invited in. Would he have been so inviting if he knew I'd taken his tarp?

"You ever ride one of these bad boys before?" he said, removing the red, white, and blue bandana from his head. His salt-and-pepper colored hair held the perfect helmet shape.

"Mom says no." I stepped forward to touch the handlebars.

"So, you must be staying with the campers in the front."

"Uh, huh."

"Climb on up."

"Sure," I said. It was a lot bigger than I thought it would be. I could touch my feet to the pegs, but I needed all of my size-10 shoe to reach my tiptoes to the ground. I leaned over the gas tank to reach the handlebars. This would not be a comfortable way to ride across the country.

"You'd grow into it."

"Thanks," I said, sliding off the seat to stand flat-footed once again.

"I'm Larry. Who are you?"

"Logan."

"Logan. Interesting name."

"Thanks."

"So, Logan, are your parents missing you?"

"Naw, they're busy setting up."

"And they don't need you to help?"

"No. They're pretty much done. See we're in that tent over there," I said trying not to point at any specific tent. Larry followed the direction of my finger.

"The red one?"

"Yeah, sure."

"Oh, you're with the Smiths. Met them this morning before our ride."

"Uh, huh, Logan Smith. That's me."

"Funny, they didn't mention having children."

"Oh, that's my folks all right. Funny people."

"They did mention grandchildren and their sixtieth wedding anniversary."

The sick feeling was coming back into my stomach.

"Come on, Logan. What's the deal?"

"No deal. I'm staying in the campground. I just got confused with all the same-colored tents."

Larry smiled and shook his head. "That's not going to work either. Everyone in this campground has been coming here for years. This is the tenth year in a row our group has come here. Everyone knows everyone.

And everyone will tell you that there has never been a Logan. So, what's the story?"

"I live in Denver and just wanted to get out and do some camping. My parents are very much into survival of the fittest and all. They encourage me and my brother to just get back to nature."

I felt the blood draining from my head. The chili and anxiety were not a good combination.

Larry leaned on his bike. "Try again."

"You want the truth?"

"Yes."

"You won't believe me."

"Try me."

"Okay. The other day was my birthday. I turned thirteen."

"Happy Birthday."

"Thanks, but that's not the point."

"Sorry, go on."

"Okay. My cousin John Michael said he was getting grandfather's watch because I was adopted. No one ever told me I was adopted. I asked David and Jill—they used to be my parents—and they confirmed it. So, I ran away to find my real parents in Fort Scott, Kansas. I bought a bus ticket, took a detour to see the Grand

Canyon, then was kidnapped by a very intense lady in Denver, lost my backpack with my money and stuff, escaped at the fast-food place up the road, walked here, made camp under there, and now I'm looking for a ride to Fort Scott."

Larry met my gaze with a blank stare.

"No, kid, really, the truth."

"That is the truth," I said. "Why do I bother? I should just stick to lying."

"Logan. You have to admit that sounds a bit made up."

I grabbed Larry by the arm. He resisted but then followed me. I lifted the skirt on the trailer and showed him my home. "See?"

"Hey, that's my tarp."

CHAPTER 19

"**U**sing chili as an escape plan, that's pretty clever," said Larry, as we headed back to the center of camp.

"Thanks. It's also pretty painful."

My stomach was churning, and my legs felt weak.

"I'll see if Doc has anything for you. Take a seat."

Larry walked to a blue tent and came back with a bottle of antacids. I wanted to eat them all but took just a couple. I washed them down with a soda. A few burps later and I was good as new.

"Yeah, you must be feeling better," Larry said. "Kid, these are a few of my friends, Larry, Larry, and Gary."

"You're kidding me, right."

"Naw."

And he wasn't.

Soon the men were all sitting in a semicircle with me, and the women were cooking dinner for the night. They all started talking at once.

"What a ride."

"That was a long drop off that one corner."

"Who's the kid?"

"I need to ride into town and get a part."

"Logan."

"What part do you need?"

"Logan. That's a funny name."

"I need to go into town for more food. I could pick up a part."

"That's what I told him."

My head spun trying to keep it all straight. I knew they were talking about me on occasion, and that someone would be headed into town. Most towns had a bus depot, so I'd need to get in on the trip.

"Dinner's ready," one of the women called. The men let out low moans as their bodies resisted getting up out of the chairs. I was firmly planted in my seat, planning my next move. "Come on, you too, boy."

"What are you eating?" I asked.

"Chili."

Now, it was my turn to let out a slow groan. I wasn't that hungry, and I definitely wasn't hungry for chili. "Thanks, but I'm still full from lunch."

"Suit yourself."

TO WHOM IT MAY CONCERN:

The men came back one at a time after filling their plates. The smell and sight of the chili was nearly too much for me. I half-covered my mouth and nose with my hand and continued to drink my soda.

"So where are you from Logan?" asked a skinny guy, whose leather vest had a giant eagle on it.

It was the only question out there. Apparently, the key to normal conversation with this group was food. They couldn't all talk when they were all eating.

"California."

"Where you headed?" asked a bearded man.

"East." I was keeping answers short to avoid breathing too much.

"He's going to Fort Scott with me," Larry said between heaping spoonfuls of chili.

"Really?" I said at the same time as the one he called Doc.

"Yeah," Larry continued. "He's traveling with the Browns. The family in the silver stream-line trailer."

"They pulled out this morning," the bearded man said.

"Right," Larry said, pointing at him with his spoon. "But before they left, they said they wanted to go up into Montana, but Logan needed to get home, so they

115

weren't going to be able. So, I asked where the boy needed to go, and they said Fort Scott. Since it's on the way back, I didn't see any trouble."

"I thought his home was California."

"No, you asked where he was coming from."

Wow, Larry was my hero. I finally found someone who was a faster storyteller than me.

"You didn't think to ask me?"

"No, Doc. I didn't think you'd mind if we had an extra person."

"I guess he can wipe down the bikes at night to earn his keep," said Doc with a smile that betrayed his kind side. "But he rides on your bike."

"That's lucky for him," said one of the ladies who had joined the circle.

Everyone joined her for a laugh. It seemed like avoiding the back of Doc's bike was a good thing. I had a place to sleep and a ride. And more than a ride, it was on a motorcycle. I'd finish my journey with the wind whipping through my air.

Suddenly there was a smack on my head and the world went black.

"Here's your helmet, kid." I couldn't see Doc, but I knew his voice. He banged on the helmet a few more times. It bobbled on my head like a dog in the back window of a car.

So much for the wind in my hair.

CHAPTER 20

"Here," said Larry, dropping a cell phone into my lap.

"What's this for," I said, holding it up to him.

"To call people. Don't you have those in California?"

"Yes, we have them. Why are you giving it to me?"

"Call your parents."

"No," I said, tossing the phone back at him.

"Fine. No call. No ride." He said as he turned around.

I jumped up from the chair and grabbed his elbow. "Let me see it."

"Take your time," he said with a mile-wide smile.

A lot had transpired since the last call.

"Hey, Rachel, it's me."

"It's good to hear your voice. Your parents have gone frantic. They didn't tell me anything specific, only that they needed a divine intervention and asked me to kick my prayers up a notch."

"How could they know?"

"Know what, dear?"

"Some lady tried to kidnap me."

"Oh, dear Lord, no."

"Yes. And now I'm traveling with a biker gang."

"Logan. The truth."

"No, really. May John Michael come live with me if I'm lying."

"A biker gang?"

"Okay, they're all older than my dad, I mean, David." The word had slipped out. It sounded comforting and foreign all at the same time. "They're taking me the rest of the way."

"Where are you going, Logan?"

"To find answers," I pulled the phone away from my ear to hit the end button but couldn't. "Rachel, you still there?"

"Yeah, I'm here."

"I miss you. Tell David and Jill and Dayton and Blue that I miss them, too."

"I will, child. I will."

"Bye."

Jill and David were running around crazed. They did care. There was a warm feeling starting to grow in my stomach and this time it wasn't from the chili.

I didn't know how they could have known I was in trouble. Maybe they had a trace on the first bus I booked to Fort Smith and freaked out after it arrived without me. Whatever it was, I was glad. It's good to be missed.

Unfortunately for me, the warm fuzzy feeling of being loved didn't keep me warm on the outside. The Colorado air caused goosebumps to grow on my bare legs and arms. The glow of the space heaters and the desires to warm up drew me back to the center of the group. They weren't allowed an open flame. Doc said something about nearly burning down a national park once. I think he was kidding.

"How'd it go?"

"Fine. Thanks, Larry," I said handing him the phone and stepping closer to the heater.

"No problem. Everything fine."

"They're starting to miss me."

"Wish I could say the same thing," Doc said, laughing at his own joke.

I wasn't sure I was going to survive the next couple days traveling with him and Larry. But then again two days on a Harley-Davidson were more than compensation for bad humor.

Huddled next to the heater, I absorbed all the stories from the day. There were close calls on gravel roads, near misses with oversized travel trailers, and breathtaking encounters on windy mountain roads. Each story got longer and more exaggerated.

These were my kind of people. They could tell one whopping lie and wrap just enough truth in there to keep you wondering if it wasn't all true. Who's to say, Doc didn't really ride a wheelie for a mile, including crossing a suspension bridge, after popping his tire when he ran over a porcupine?

"My turn."

"Okay, California boy, give it a try."

"One morning, I got up while it was still dark and ran to the beach. The waves were rolling smooth and steady; it was perfect. I paddled out and caught the first wave. I rode that thing all the way down the coast and eased on to the sand. It was so amazing I went out to do it again. This time, I caught what I thought was another awesome wave, but it started to cave in on me. I ducked down as it crashed on my head. I looked over at the wall of water and a dolphin was staring at me. He gave me a tap and knocked me off my board, and I tumbled in the surf."

TO WHOM IT MAY CONCERN:

They were all staring at me. I was pretty sure I'd used small enough words even for bikers to understand.

"I don't believe it." Doc said.

"What it's true. There are most-excellent waves and dolphins."

"Oh, I believe that. I don't believe any kid gets up before dawn."

CHAPTER 21

ikers have a hard time getting up before dawn, also.

I crawled out from under the trailer about an hour after the sun crawled over the mountains. My back sounded liked a bowl of crisped cereal, popping as I straightened up.

One of the wives, I think her name was Mary, was busy frying bacon. It smelled wonderful.

There was no sign of Larry or the Doc. Their bikes were still parked neatly by their tents, so they were around somewhere.

"You hungry?"

"Yeah, I could eat," I said walking toward her.

"Here cut these up for me," she said, tossing me a potato. "There's more over there."

I stared at the potato and looked around for a knife.

"Knife's over there," she said pointing with her elbow as she pushed her hair back with her hand. "Slice 'em like chips."

The first slices were thick chips, but I got better as I went on. I heard tents being zipped open and knew the others were getting up for the day. I didn't look up because I was afraid my fingers would become one of the chips.

"Hey, kid, you're pretty good at that," Doc said. "You can cook for us on the road."

Doc's perpetual smile made it hard to tell when he was joking or being serious.

Something told me that I was going to do a major portion of the chores between here and Fort Scott. I hoped Larry drove fast.

"You ready to go?" said Larry, who had a towel draped around his neck. "How 'bout you, Doc?"

"I'm good," said Doc, "I showered the other day."

"We'll ride ahead of him, won't we," I asked Larry.

"Way ahead," he said with a smile.

I didn't have anything to pack, but I did re-distribute what I had borrowed for the night. Not one person yelled at me, but they didn't look too pleased either.

"Saddle up, boy."

"What about breakfast?" I asked.

"Grab a few pieces of bacon."

I downed the greasy strips and climbed up on the back of Larry's bike. The back seat looked like an overstuffed recliner and was just as comfortable. I pulled the helmet on and felt suddenly claustrophobic. It was heavy and made my neck hurt.

"You okay?" Larry's voice echoed around in my ears and the helmet.

"Wow, that's loud."

Larry showed me the volume controls.

"Trouble over there?" came Doc's voice.

I turned to see him on his bike at the end of the driveway, waiting by the road.

"I can hear him?"

"Yep."

"Does this have a mute?"

"Very funny kid. For that, I'm not buying you ice cream when we stop at the Dairy Queen."

Larry sighed into the microphone. "This is going to be a long trip."

Within seconds, we were on the road. Before I could get hungry again, we had crossed the Colorado border into Kansas.

"Hey, we're almost there, huh?"

Larry shook his helmet.

"We just started, and he's already asking if we're there yet."

"Stop it, Doc. Just because he beat you to it."

Aside from the occasional passing car, Kansas offered little excitement for me. As far as I could see through the slit in the helmet there were fields and fields and fields.

I listened to Larry and Doc recall various trips through Kansas. Their stories would make good fertilizer. After a while, I unplugged my helmet and heard just the wind and engine of the motorcycle. The combination made me sleepy, and I propped my head back just to take a nap.

The sudden snapping forward of my head woke me up.

It was quiet. The bike was in the parking lot of a Dairy Queen. Doc walked out with a chocolate dipped cone. I slipped the helmet off. The breeze cooled my face.

"You decide to wake up Sleeping Beauty?"

"Where's Larry?"

"Inside. Hurry and you can catch him. He may even buy you something."

I hopped off and ran toward the building. I pushed the doors open and nearly plastered a man walking out with two swirl cones.

"Sorry, mister."

"Dumb kid," he said, slipping out the door.

Larry was standing next to the counter. I walked up to him.

"You like hamburgers?"

I nodded.

"Good. I got you one."

The lady handed him a bag and we started out. I turned to see the man and his child licking their ice cream cones.

"Here, go get one," said Larry, handing me some money.

"Thanks, a lot," I said and ran back in.

I walked back out with my chocolate-dipped swirl cone. It tasted great. No matter where you were, ice cream tastes great.

"Eat it before you get on."

I looked over at Doc, happily eating his cone on his bike.

"I have better manners than him."

"What?" said Doc, who had a smattering of chocolate on his shirt.

"True, get on. We'll try to make some extra distance."

Three more ice-cream stops and a very sore butt later, we pulled into a campground for the night. I hobbled to the tent. Turns out if I'd looked hard enough the night before I would have found Larry's extra one-man tent. I pitched it between him and Doc. I tossed and turned as they snored.

I needed that mute button now.

CHAPTER 22

"Tornado," I yelled, as my tent was lifted from the ground causing me to slide down to the end. I fumbled with the zipper. "Larry! Doc! Help me!"

Doc's laughter overpowered my screams for help. I slipped my head out from the opening and saw him holding the other end of the tent up in the air.

"Rise and shine, little man. Time to hit the road."

"What? The sun's not even up yet."

"Larry wants to hit Fort Scott early. Think he's in a hurry to get you back to your family, so we can get back home."

"Put the tent down, Doc," Larry said as he folded his gear.

Doc dropped the tent. I pulled the sleeping bag out with me and started rolling it up.

"You really in a hurry to get rid of me," I said. "You don't want me around?"

Larry continued to look at the equipment. "I'm in a hurry to get on the road. I don't mind you at all. But I figured you'd be in a hurry to find your family."

"Yeah, I guess."

"You having second thoughts," he said as he came over to help me tie up the tent.

Truth was I was having second, third, fourth, and fifth thoughts. I wasn't so angry with Jill and David anymore, which left room for other emotions to come flooding into my head.

Now, the eagerness to find out who I am was turning to anxiety about who I might find. Instead of asking, "Why would Jill and David lie to me?" I was asking, "Why would someone leave me in a hospital with a note?"

"I'm okay, Larry. Thanks for asking."

"All right then. Saddle up."

Sleeping on the hard ground made the start of the day's ride even worse. I didn't think my butt could get any sorer.

Larry fired up the motorcycle, and we were headed for Fort Scott. Five hours from the truth.

Turns out with Doc five hours is more like seven by the time you factor in all the ice-cream stops. He ate more ice cream than his bike drank gas.

TO WHOM IT MAY CONCERN:

The plains eventually gave way to rolling hills. I was still sore but at least the scenery had changed. I was beginning to think we were never going to get there.

"There it is, kid," came Doc's voice through my helmet.

It didn't look any different than any of the other towns we'd passed through. Sitting up on a bluff above the river, the brick buildings looked like something out of an Old West movie. We crossed the bridge with its tall towers and were in downtown. It was technically the old downtown, a lot of the stores moved or closed after the Wal-Mart opened "down the way."

"Let's get some lunch," Doc said.

"Where do you put it all?" asked Larry.

"Come on. Race you." Doc revved his engine.

Larry nodded. My head was slammed back at the sudden burst of speed.

"Where are we racing to?"

"Lunch."

"He didn't say where." I grabbed hold of any part of the bike that seemed stable.

"We always eat at the best place in town," Doc said.

A few quick turns and the ride was over. Doc was leaning against his bike.

"Guess that means we lost," I said, taking off the helmet.

"It makes him feel good, so I let him win," Larry said.

"Liar. Just for that I'm going to let you buy me lunch."

"Like that wasn't going to happen anyway."

They argued all the way into the Main Street Chop House and Bar-B-Que. They continued to argue as we seated ourselves at a table. It was obvious to me I wasn't going to get a word in any time soon, so I read the menu. I'd decided on the chicken and rib combo, when Doc and Larry decided they'd split the check.

The restaurant was nearly full. The waitress greeted everyone who came in after us by name. She asked one couple how their grandmother was doing after falling off the porch, another family caught her up on their vacation to Florida—they even brought her a gift.

So, this was small-town America, this is where I'm from; these were my people. If my real mother would have stayed around, the waitress (who I learned was named Susan) would have said, "Hey, Logan, you want the usual?" when I walked in. But she didn't stick around, and I didn't have a usual. Susan walked to our table.

"What can I get for—oh, my, goodness, Doc and Larry, it's so great to see you. Who's your friend?"

"His name is Logan," Larry said. "It's good to see you, too. We'll take the usual, and the boy will have the chicken and ribs."

"I'll get that right up."

Country music poured from a boombox sitting on a table at the front of the restaurant. These couldn't be my people. However, the restaurant had a homey feel to it. It may have been the seafoam green paint on the walls. It was very peaceful against the hardwood. There were pictures showing the town in various stages since before the Civil War.

"After lunch, will you take me to the hospital?" I asked Larry.

"You sick, kid?" Doc asked.

I glanced at Doc and then looked at Larry. "Please."

"Are you sure?"

I nodded.

"Okay, right after we eat."

The food arrived quickly and went down Doc's throat even faster. We were waiting for the bill when Susan told Larry this one was on her.

"Thanks. What's the best way to get to the hospital?"

"Hey, don't ask that question in here after eating. People will get the wrong message," she said, smacking Larry on the shoulder. "They closed the old one down. The new one's up on the hill."

"Thanks," he said. Loudly, he added, "This is the best food I've ever had."

People in the restaurant laughed and nodded their agreement.

CHAPTER 23

"I'll drop you off and come back to get you. Then we'll put you on a plane home."

Home. I had traveled halfway across the country to find my home. I left a shimmering ocean with sounds and smells that made me feel alive to come to a place with sounds and smells that made me feel out of place.

"That's okay. I'll stick around here for a while."

We pulled up in front of the hospital.

"You will call home. You will go home."

"Thanks for the ride, but you are not the boss of me. I don't need your help. Just leave me like everyone."

I dropped the helmet in the seat and ran inside. I heard the motorcycles drive away.

The smell in the hospital was worse than outside. I hated the smell. It alone made me sick. It, plus what I was about to do, had my stomach turning 360s.

"Can I help you?" asked the lady behind the counter. The name plate in front of her said Betty Washington. It should have read: Warning, way too much perfume.

I wasn't really sure what I needed.

"I was born here, and I need a copy of my birth certificate with my mother's name."

"Where is your mother?"

"I was hoping you could tell me."

"Are you lost?" she said and grabbed the phone. "Let me get security."

"No. I'm not lost. I'm adopted."

"Oh, I see. You need your parents' consent to fill out paperwork. Are they parking the car?"

"No. I'm here by myself. I didn't want to hurt them."

It was the biggest lie I'd told since, well, ever. I did want to hurt them. They had hurt me, and it only seemed fair. But saying it out loud made me sound mean instead of justified.

"Look. Thirteen years ago, a runaway left a baby here with a note. That's me. So, now I want to know why."

"Oh, my, the bus baby. The bus baby, oh my. You're famous."

"Great for me. I was born on a bus."

"Yes." She punched buttons on the phone. "Claire, you'll never guess who's here. No, not her. The bus baby . . . No, I'm not kidding."

I heard fast walking from down a hallway and assumed Claire was on her way to catch a glimpse of the bus baby. I could have been part of those sideshows we passed earlier in the state. See the world's largest prairie dog and the bus baby.

"Oh, you're so cute," Claire said. "Isn't he just so cute, Betty?"

"Can either of you help me find my mother?"

"Why don't you come with me. We can talk in my office."

I didn't want to talk, but Claire's office at least got me away from Betty's overpowering perfume.

"Have a seat. Do you need anything to drink?"

"No. I'm just 'thirsty for the truth' as my grandpa would say."

She didn't really have much information. All she knew of that day thirteen years ago was that there was a frantic cell phone call from a bus. A young woman was going into labor. By the time the bus got into town, I was born. They took my mother and me in on a stretcher. When they went to check on her, they just found a note. They tried to track her down, but the name she used was fake. The next thing they knew a couple from California was going to adopt the baby. Case closed.

"Do you still have the note?"

"No. It was part of files that were accidentally destroyed when we moved from the old hospital."

"I came all this way for nothing."

"If you came, maybe she will."

"I don't understand."

"We'll have you write a note for her. We'll put it in a file, and if, when, she comes to see what became of you, she'll get the note."

Claire walked me back to the front and told Betty to find me a room where I wouldn't be bothered. That didn't seem like it would be possible with Betty, she bothered me no matter where I was.

I tried to remember how my teachers taught us to write letters: *Dear Mr. or Mrs. So-and-So.* That didn't feel right. *To whom it may concern.* Now, that felt more like it.

But that's as far as I got. Betty hounded me outside and thoughts of Jill and David hounded me from the inside. They might not be my real parents, but they never left me alone to fend for myself. They traveled halfway across the country to choose me.

Maybe they didn't tell me because they were afraid that I wouldn't choose them back. There were times when I had gotten really ticked off that I told Jill and David I wished they weren't my parents.

Maybe they didn't tell me because they were afraid this would happen.

Going back to a place where I knew I was loved, regardless of if they were my "real" family, suddenly seemed much better than being in a place where I'm the bus baby.

My head hurt.

I stuffed the paper in my pocket and left. I could feel Betty's eyes burning a hole in the back of my head as I walked out. I could hear her talking to people, but the only words I could make out were "bus baby."

The doors slid open, and I was greeted by the fresh Kansas air. I wasn't sure where to go. I didn't see Doc or Larry. I had told them to take off, so I shouldn't be surprised that they did. I decided to head back toward the old town, at least people there were friendly. I nearly tripped over the outstretched legs of a man sitting on a bench.

"Where are you going?"

"Hey, your legs were in the way," I said, turning to see a strangely familiar face. "Warden?"

"Been waiting for you, Logan." My former bus driver, Bob, didn't even wince at being called Warden.

"Waiting for me? Why would you be waiting for me?"

"Take a seat."

"Why does everyone want me to sit? I've been sitting all day. I'll stand for you if that's okay?"

"Sure. It's kind of a long story, but I'll shorten it. I was the driver when you were born."

I sat down beside him.

"Thought that might get your attention. It was the cross-country run, nearly the same one you took. Kind of funny that way, huh?"

I didn't see the humor.

"Anyway, all those years back, I thought there might be trouble when we started out of LA. What with her looking like she had a basketball tucked under her shirt."

I grabbed his shoulder. "What did you say?"

"A basketball under . . . "

"No, before that. Where did she start from?"

"LA Like you. Don't you remember me saying you took nearly the same route?"

"My parents said I was from Kansas."

"You were born in Kansas."

"But she was from California, so I *am* Californian."

"I believe she was actually from the East Coast. She had a ticket all the way to Boston."

"Did she get back on the bus after the hospital?"

"I don't know. I was busy calling your parents; we'd been friends forever. I wanted to tell them about the little miracle on my bus. People were already calling you the bus baby and growing up in a small town is tough enough without being labeled from the get-go."

"You know my parents, *um*, Jill and David."

"Yeah from college. I was just a driver back then, but I've been in upper management for years now. Haven't really driven a bus in a while. But they called me the night you learned the truth. They were afraid you may do something crazy, like running away. They emailed me a picture of you, and we decided if you showed up at the station, I'd drive whatever bus you got a ticket for. We figured it would be a good way to keep an eye on you."

"You were spying on me."

"Yeah, the Grand Canyon detour threw me. I flew to Denver. When you didn't get on the bus in Denver. I knew there was trouble."

"Dude, yeah, that lady was taking me home as her long lost son. I barely escaped, and then I hooked up with the motorcycle gang . . . "

"Whoa, your parents said you had quite an imagination."

"Why do I even bother attempting to tell the truth?"

The deep roar of Doc and Larry's bikes caught my ears. They pulled up, and I waved them over.

"Well, I'll be . . . " Bob said.

"Couldn't leave me?"

"I would have but Larry insisted we check up on you." Doc didn't hide his smile.

"Thanks," I said. "Larry, Doc, this is Bob the bus driver. He delivered me when I was born."

"Did you even try to put him back?" Doc said.

Larry stared him down. "Knock it off, Marvin."

"Marvin?" I laughed. "I'd go by Doc, too."

"You taking him back to California?" Larry asked.

"No, I have people to do that." He pointed toward a blue van. Jill and David stepped out from the side door. Dayton squeezed from behind them and ran ahead.

"Dayton." His name nearly stuck in my throat. I ran toward him and gave him a bear hug.

Jill and David stopped running a step away. Our eyes locked. The days apart now seemed like a lifetime. A few days ago, I thought of us as magnets pushing each other apart, now that charge had shifted, and I was drawn to them.

"Mom. Dad . . . I'm . . . "

"We know son." Dad pulled us all together for a family hug. "We know."

I pushed away. "No, you don't know. I'm not sorry for running away. I'm not sorry for wanting to know the truth, but I am sorry that you were upset. I'm sorry that I don't have any answers . . . The papers they did have were destroyed."

"I'm sorry, Logan," Mom said, brushing away tears.

"Me too, kid." Larry walked over to meet us.

"Mom, Dad, Dayton. This is Larry, my motorcycle buddy."

"Motorcycle buddy?" Mom asked.

"Yes, ma'am. Logan, Doc." He pointed over at Doc who nodded his head, "and I rode together from just outside Denver to here the last two days."

"You were on a motorcycle?" Mom's face was getting red, and Dad was laughing.

"You are in serious trouble."

"I wore a helmet."

EPILOGUE

"**N**o surfing for a month? You might as well kill me."

My parents stood shoulder-to-shoulder in our living room. There was not going to be a debate.

I thought being abducted by C.B. and developing an iron butt from riding a motorcycle would have been punishment enough. However, it seemed with every new thing I told my parents, they wanted to add on to my punishment. It was wise to quit while there would still be some summer left.

"Son . . . "

"Yeah, I know. It's for my own good."

I headed for my room; each step weighed on my feet like thick mud. I was home. The beach was right outside. But I had to serve out my sentence. There was a new warden in my life—two of them actually.

I opened the window to let the sound and smell of the ocean overflow my room. My bed felt comfortable after all the bus seats and camping.

"It's good to have you home," Dayton said, peeking around the door.

I motioned for him to come in and take a seat.

He pulled out a box from under his shirt. "You never opened your gift from Mom and Dad."

"Do they know you have it?"

"No," he laughed. "Open it."

"Are you trying to get me in trouble?"

"Dude, you're already in so deep, what's one more?"

"And they say I'm the bad influence."

I took the box and tore the paper. The shredding sounded so much better in my ears than the slight whisper of sneaking a peak. I took the lid off the little white box.

"Cool, Logan, a diver's watch."

"It's way cool." I slipped it on my wrist. "And just think, in thirty days I'll actually be able to get it wet."

ACKNOWLEDGEMENTS

As an adopted child, a huge thanks go to my parents, Gerry and Nickie, for adopting and loving me, and for not asking for a refund. (FYI: I'm one of a few kids that has a receipt from the lawyer in their baby book.) I am thankful I finished this novel before my dad died in June 2022 and that I was able to read it to him and my mom.

Also thanks to my biological units for making the tough call to place me up for adoption.

My adoption story is nothing like Logan's. I've known my entire life that I was adopted. However, I've had many friends who were adopted and learned from them the pain and confusion that comes from learning later in life about being adopted. As a native Californian, I channeled my imagination into what would it be like to lose that identity.

I want to thank JuLee Brand for believing in this story. I'm proud to be part of the Idun imprint of W. Brand Publishing.

Thanks to the myriad friends who have encouraged me, with a special hat tip to Emma, David, Chandrika, Chris, Leah, Shan, Laura, and Michael. They provided feedback, swift kicks, and unconditional love.

This has been a rough time with the passing of my dad, and I have learned the strength of family. For all the extra love and care, thanks to my aunts and uncles (Earl, Ann, Jim, Gary, Pam, Dale, Debbie, Victor; Wayne, Margie, Frank, Nancy) and numerous cousins.

Shout out to all my road tripping buddies. It wasn't enough for me to look at a map and plot a course. I've driven or been a passenger on ninety percent of the distance covered by Logan. Thanks to Lynette for planning a trip to Colorado, where I met her amazing parents, Larry and Carol, who introduced me to their "biker gang" that inspired the spirited riders of this story.

There is an actual Fort Scott, Kansas, and I have been there and enjoyed the amazing hospitality it had to offer, including a meal at the Main Street Chop House and Bar-B-Que. (Sadly, it reportedly closed.) I met so many amazing people along my travels who show up in various forms in the story. However, the Crying Bus lady is one hundred percent made up.

ABOUT THE AUTHOR

Kim Orendor was adopted at two-and-a-half months old and grew up in Southern California, riding bicycles, skateboards, and motorcycles. She grew up knowing she was adopted. It was a very different story than some of her friends, who didn't find out until later in life that they were adopted, and it upended their worlds.

She often wondered what her life would have been like if she had learned about her adoption from someone other than her parents. How would she react? How would she feel? That curiosity coupled with her love of storytelling led to the book you now hold in your hands.

Before writing books—this is her second—Kim honed her writing craft as a sports reporter. She's clocked more than twenty years of experience between

The Sacramento Bee and *The Davis Enterprise*. At *The Enterprise*, she won state and national writing awards and was the sports editor in charge of multiple state and national award-winning sections.

Kim's career path took a dramatic turn in 2006 when she began a five-year teaching stint at Sias International University in China's Henan Province. The administration took advantage of her experience, and she taught newspaper and reading classes. She was later thrilled to get to teach American Culture Through Film, where she learned the universal secrets behind storytelling. This led to her first book, a memoir *Unbound Feet: Finding Freedom in Communist China*, also with W. Brand Publishing.

Kim returned to the Sacramento area in 2018 to be a caretaker for her parents. Her dad, a Navy veteran, was diagnosed with a rare neurological disease. Sadly, he passed in 2022, but not before Kim was able to finish this novel and read it aloud to him and her mom. Kim continues to live in Northern California with her mom.

DISCUSSION QUESTIONS

1. When Logan learns he's adopted, how does he react in the moment? Have you ever received news that caused you to feel the same way? If you feel safe in sharing, please, let the group know what happened and how you dealt with it.

2. The major theme of the story is family. How did the author show that? There are also minor themes, including trust and friendship. Can you find others? Please, give examples to support your idea.

3. Of all the characters in the book, who would you like to have lunch with and why?

4. Pick two characters and describe their relationship. Use examples from the story to show how they feel about each other.

5. How does Logan handle the various situations he gets into along the journey? How would you have handled a similar situation?

6. Logan has lived in Southern California his whole life. What surprises him as he travels away from home? What are some things you enjoy about where you live? If you've taken a trip, what did you learn about other parts of your state/country on your journey?

7. This book is set in 1995. How would it be different if it were to happen today?

8. What part of the story stands out most in your memory? How would you turn this into a television show or movie? What actors would you cast to play the parts? What type of music would be playing to set the mood? If you are working in groups, create a script and act out part of the scene.